THE LAST VOYAGE OF MRS. COLDING

LAIR
5

D.V. SULLIVAN

TRANSMARINIA PRESS

Transmarinia Press
2709 N Hayden Island Dr
STE 330550
Portland, OR 97217

*They choose us
because we're strong*

PROLOGUE

It can't be.

I lift the binoculars again to glass the hot night. And there it is, beyond all reasoning. That superyacht that resembles a Chinese junk. Its jagged red sails unfurl like dragon's wings as it hoves out of the blurry waves of heat, the flames dancing over the grave of the recently sunken Castle Volok on the South China Sea. And I see him.

My ears ring. My scalp crawls. My hands grow clammy with sweat.

It can't be. It doesn't make sense.

This cannot be.

My plan, miraculously, had worked. Somehow, I had rescued Captain Redfearn before he could sacrifice himself for his daughter's life, dragged him out of the obsidian-black hell of Castle Volok and ignited the charges I'd stuck to the fortress's pylons. The harebrained scheme had been more spectacularly successful than I'd even dared imagine. The one-kiloton payload had crumpled those pylons as if by the sudden crushing weight of the deep and sunk the castle below the waves, its veins of green phosphor pulsing an eerie and dying morse code. But not before a boat had escaped from its bowels.

His boat.

And he's there now. That figure at the bow that should not be there. That man whose impossible existence is threatening my sense of reality. After all these years, he looks unchanged, as if not a day has gone by. The same high forehead and contemptuous but weak lips. The same commanding eyes. The same dark widow's peak, contrasting with skin that now has a corpselike pallor to it. He's wearing—of course—a Chinese robe that whips in the wind, its shimmery purple gleaming with patterns of hypnotic scales and the plunging jaws of dragons.

Except, I can't see his eyes. Because something is covering them. Something sinister-looking. It looks like goggles, black and rounded. Like two grotesque, alien knobs.

Binoculars.

He's also looking through binoculars. Looking straight at me.

He's seen me.

A cold hand plunges inside my chest, squeezes my heart.

And the Steward of Castle Volok lowers the binoculars so he can lift a bullhorn to his lips.

"Hello, my little empress," the bullhorn blares, the words carrying clear and lazy through the spark-filled night. And it is the final, necessary piece. That cripplingly familiar voice, with all its intonations of intimacy and menace, that allows that trauma to lay its claim on me once more. To tumble me back, back, back into that dark era, long ago, when I called him husband, and he called me wife.

And I remember.

PART ONE:

COLDING MANSION

ONE

"I thought you'd be tired."

"What?"

I blinked and tore my eyes away from the properties of Fort Lauderdale's multimillionaires gliding past my window. It was all so different in America. The soaring opulence of the houses. The shapes of yachts glinting along the canals. The air of freedom and possibility.

I was finally here.

"After such a long flight," my driver clarified. "Sixteen hours from Hong Kong?"

In my distraction, I'd hardly noticed my driver. I studied him then in the rearview mirror. Hispanic, with strong, stubborn cheekbones, smooth skin almost flawless. He must have been no more than twenty-five. Just a couple of years older than me, though he looked like he'd barely grown out of boyhood, still left with that gangliness I always thought had a certain innocence about it. When he glanced at me in the mirror, I caught the flash of his eyes. Kind, but reserved. Wary, perhaps.

He'd said his name was Miguel.

"I guess I'm excited," I said, turning back to the window. "Maybe a little nervous."

He grunted as he turned the gleaming black Range Rover onto a more private street. "Mr. Colding can do that."

I swallowed, the mention of his name throwing me back into the past. I remembered the day my father introduced me to him, a strange American visiting Hong Kong on a business venture, and who had hired my father to give him a tour of the bay. His attention had made me feel like I was the center of the world, his intense gaze making me blush in an instant. I remembered our long walks along Kowloon Bay and telling him about fishing with my father, the antics of my friends at school, my aspirations to see the world, stories I would later look back on as mortifyingly inane and childish. But that did not stop him from asking, almost dizzyingly shortly thereafter, for my father's permission to marry me.

I glanced down at the ring on my hand. It was huge, of white gold, with the biggest diamond I had ever seen. It glittered and flashed like a hundred crystal worlds on my finger, dazzling me.

I swallowed and smoothed the skirt of my traditional qipao with its rich swirl of designs.

"Don't worry."

I jerked my head up. Miguel was watching me in the mirror.

His mouth crooked in a kind and almost sad smile. "You look very beautiful."

An unexpected heat crept up my neck, into my cheeks. Feeling suddenly bold, I tossed my head and lifted my chin. "Do you think he'll like my hair?" I asked, pulling it in front of my shoulders.

I loved my hair. It was my favorite thing about me. I'd gotten it from my mother—silky and dark as the princesses in my father's folktales. Every night I brushed it and put it up into a bun so it wouldn't be damaged, only to unleash it in the morning, feel it flow long and free behind me in the wind on my father's fishing boat. I thought of myself when I was old, with hair still beautiful, still the treasure of my husband. I had taken great care to stop in the airport bathroom to brush it again until it was sleek and shining, almost as bright as my engagement ring.

"Well?" I asked, still waiting.

Miguel stared at me a long time in the mirror, an enigmatic look in his eyes.

Then he turned away.

"It's very beautiful," he said.

The Range Rover slowed to a stop in front of huge wrought-iron gates set into a high cement wall lined with palm trees, and I looked up at them. Their two halves met to form something inside a circle: the letter C, with a fancy curlicue at the top.

And I knew, with a drop in my stomach, that we'd arrived at Colding Mansion.

I lifted my eyes above the gates.

The mansion was like a castle. High and grand, with many windows, many palm trees about it. But it was not cold, as the name of Colding would suggest. It was an explosion of color, its terracotta roof tiles bloodred, its rose stucco façade almost fantastical in the baking heat. Bougainvillea grew up its turrets and wrought-iron balconies in a riot of pink blooms, bees buzzing among their heady scents. And its yard was a delirium of azaleas bordering the cement driveway in thick brambles of pink and purple.

"This is where I leave you," Miguel said with a new curtness, hands whitening on the wheel. "I have to run some errands for Mr. Colding."

"Thank you." I slipped out the door, turned toward the trunk.

But Miguel leaned out his window.

"You needn't worry about that," he said back to me, not quite looking at me. "I'll bring your bags up when I return."

"Oh." I turned warm with embarrassment. "Okay."

He stilled at that, as if sensing my self-consciousness, and lifted his eyes to me, an almost stern kindness in them returning. "If you ever need anything, señora, just ask."

"Thank you, Miguel," I said, and smiled.

After a moment, he flickered his eyes away, stuck a remote out the window and clicked.

In a low whine of electric motors, the immense wrought-iron gates began to swing inward, halving that fancy C at their top and beckoning me inside.

When I turned back, Miguel was gone, the Range Rover already fading in the blurry waves of heat radiating off the asphalt road.

Leaving me alone.

Swallowing, I strode down the driveway to Colding Mansion.

With every step, it grew taller, broader, shouldering up against the blazing sky. I couldn't believe it. I couldn't believe that such a place would be my home. I felt buoyed up, enchanted. I had tumbled into a fairytale. This place was a fairytale.

I had been rescued from my life.

At the stoop, I stopped. Marble columns soared on either side of me. The door itself seemed an entrance for giants.

Lifting my hand, I knocked on the hard polished wood.

I was shivering at this point, a fine sweat along my hairline. I brushed hastily at the dew on my cheeks, smoothed my skirt, tried to calm my breathing.

Everything hummed. The azaleas, the bougainvillea with their drooping blooms, bees crawling in and out of them. Their buzzing crowded my ears.

Very faint, I heard it. Footsteps approaching the door.

Suddenly, doubt crashed into my mind. What if I would disappoint him, find he had regretted his decision? What if I was not as pretty as he remembered? What if he preferred an American wife?

What if he would open the door, and send me away?

And then it was happening. The handle was turning, the door swinging inward to reveal a slice of impenetrable darkness. And then he was looming out of that darkness, tall, handsome, even more handsome than I remembered, with that deep V of a widow's peak, those almost paralyzing eyes.

I held my breath.

"Hello, my little empress," he said, his teeth glinting in a grin, and all the air rushed out of my lungs as I leapt into his arms.

TWO

We made straight for the bedroom.

I could barely make out what it looked like inside Colding Mansion, barely cared. I got a sense of cold marble, echoing emptiness, tall curtains drawn to shut out all light. But we had other things on our minds. We grabbed each other's hand and ran toward the sweeping staircase leading up into the gloom, cackling like children. I couldn't see where I was going. I bumped into a statue, perhaps a suit of armor, and giggled. Then he was sweeping me up into his arms, and I shrieked and hung onto his neck as he carried me, like the bride I was, up the stairs.

The bedroom was dark, too, mercifully so. I was so nervous. Hushed and trembling with yearning, but nervous to the brink of terrified.

Oh, how I wanted to please him.

The bed was wide, its sheets deep. I felt as if I was sinking into them, into another world.

But he was there, on top of me. His weight comforting me, driving me mad.

There in the dark, we whispered secrets to each other.

"Is this your first time?"

I nodded my head, solemn as a schoolgirl.

"It's okay," he said, kissing my brow, my jaw, his mouth going down me, gracing my whole body, until he was between my legs. "I'll take care of you."

A sweet and urgent pain, and then I was clinging to him, trembling, pleading for more. "Please," I whispered, my mouth at his neck, tugging at his earlobe, my hands pulling him deeper inside me as if I could meld us into one. "Please."

He was patient with me, attentive, both tender and amused as he studied my reactions to his administrations. He was not rough, as my girlfriends at school had warned me men would be. There was no brutalness, no vulgar pounding. No. He took his time, teasing me, easing in and out, torturously slow. A slick rocking of his hips with his stomach pressed against mine, so close it was unbearable. I could not stand it. I whimpered and bowed up, urging him on. Urging him faster, deeper, until I was stiffening and crying out under him, rocked by waves of inexpressible pleasure. All of me was tingling, going numb. I could feel it in my cheeks, my hands. My hands, of themselves, curled inward into fists, so tight he had to pry them open again finger by finger, laughing as he did so. I was not embarrassed, not ashamed. I felt blessed, poured full of bliss. I was floating in that bed. I was safe.

I drew him down on top of me, curling my fingers in his hair, tracing them in lazy designs along his back, whispering into his ear.

Husband. My love. My love.

Afterward, we lay there on our sides facing each other, heads propped on hands, as intimate as inmates.

"When will we marry?"

"But we already did."

I pushed him. "You know what I mean. A proper wedding."

His mouth crooked in a smile. "Soon. My business—it's been a whirlwind lately."

I scratched at a fold in the sheets. "And then there's our honeymoon."

His laughter was soft and infuriatingly charming. "That, too."

"What did you have in mind?"

"I was thinking somewhere in China."

My chest fluttered with a thrill. "Really?"

His eyes gleamed in the dark. "We could see your father in Hong Kong. Then there's someplace near there I've been wanting to see."

"Someplace?"

He nodded. "Where fire meets the sea," he intoned, as if reciting a poem, then traced his hand down my side, following the curve of my hip, making me shiver.

"Fine," I said, slapping his hand away. "Be mysterious."

He chuckled, then turned mock solemn, leaning in close. "Ready to see my baby?"

My stomach dropped. "Your baby?"

"A Sunseeker Predator," he announced, waving a hand.

It bobbed in a canal behind Colding Mansion. A gleaming white 30-foot cruiser yacht, sleek and mean as her name. He hopped onto the swim deck and offered a hand, helped me aboard.

"This is what we'll take on our honeymoon," he said, leading me up the stairs onto the aft deck and inside. "We'll ship her over on a transport boat, meet her in Hong Kong. Then go wherever we want." He waved a hand that took in the polished wood interior, the lounge, the gleaming cockpit with its navigation console. "Not a bad upgrade from your father's little fishing boat, eh?"

I pushed him, a smile curling my lips despite myself. "I like my father's little boat."

He grinned and led me to the cockpit, spreading his hands over the console as he explained the boat's specs. How fast she went, how far, what price he paid for her. I didn't follow. The words themselves faded away as I listened to the pitch of his voice, the intent look on his face. There was nothing like watching a man lose himself in some passion and become almost forgetful of you, so intent is he in his work. Nothing like it to stir the blood. Already, I knew, we were going to make love again, there on that boat, and the knowledge—the security of that fact—made me patient, dutiful, shimmering with contentment.

At last, when his explanation lapsed into silence and he turned to me, I slid my arms around his neck. "You lured me out here just so you could have your baby aboard your baby, didn't you?"

My husky tone, my unapologetic forthrightness, ignited a smoldering in his eyes. "Mmhmm."

"You like my dress?"

He nodded, looking down at my body in the qipao. "Mmhmm."

"You like your Chinese girl, don't you?"

"Mm*hmm*."

I drifted my lips close to his, whispering it. "Your Chinese wife."

"My wife," he echoed, the words plumping me up with pleasure, and I closed my eyes as we kissed.

"I have a business meeting here at the house today," he told me later as we pulled our clothes back on. "I was wondering if you could drop by during the meeting, distract them all with your ravishing beauty so I can get an edge in the proceedings."

I snorted, curling my fingers into his shirt as I hovered tauntingly in front of his face. "Whatever my husband wants."

He smirked, his eyes drifting down. "You'll have to change."

I followed his gaze, feeling a twinge of self-consciousness. "I thought you liked my qipao."

"I do," he soothed in a low voice, placing his thumb on my bottom lip. "But that's for me and me alone."

A delicious thrill, hot and satisfied, filled my body. I dropped my eyes in a flutter of lashes. "If you wish."

He laughed. And then his hand was lifting, tucking my hair behind my ear, feeling its silkiness between two fingers, and my breath caught.

He's going to say it now, I thought. *He's going to compliment my hair. His treasure.*

"You know," he said, in a light and almost indifferent tone, "your hair would look good if it was up."

When we walked back inside, my husband drew back the curtains as tall as castle banners. Late afternoon light streamed in, flooding Colding Mansion and revealing all its soaring marble grandness. It took the breath away. And now that it was no longer dark, I could see that the house was not as empty as I'd thought. There were antiquities strategically placed on marble pedestals about the place, some encased in glass. My husband caught me looking and waved a hand. "What I spend my money on. My true love."

And they *were* lovely. Vases emblazoned with flaming dragons. Suits of ceremonial armor glimmering with gold-leaf designs. A gorgeous crown for a Ming dynasty empress.

They were all from China.

My scalp prickled with a chill.

"I'll see you soon," my husband called over his shoulder as he ascended the stairs.

The meeting was held in the foyer. There was a long table there for business purposes, and my husband sat in a loose white shirt and shorts at its middle while a dozen men in suits leaned in around him, hanging on his every word.

I listened to their voices echo and bounce around the mansion for a long time, standing around the corner by the staircase. I had changed into one of my Western dresses, a sleek purple bodycon dress that hugged every curve and showed a lot of back. As I dithered, I inspected myself in a mirror on the wall, pulling at my hair and touching up my lipstick.

My hands were shaking.

When I heard the conversation move on to negotiating a price, I plucked up the courage and sauntered around the corner into the foyer.

The voices stopped. All that could be heard was the clicking of my heels in that hall. I could feel every eye on me. My body, my face, my long and bouncing hair.

Rounding the table, I leaned to place a kiss on my husband's lips. "Going out for a walk," I purred. "I'll see you later, dear."

His eyes blazed up at me, proud and possessive.

I was glowing as I straightened and began to saunter away, and the clicking of my heels faltered as I glanced out the window.

Miguel stood out in the yard, sweaty and garden clippers in hand, watching me through the window.

His face had no expression in it. No judgment. But as I walked on, my cheeks flamed with an unplaceable shame.

That night, my husband had me wear my qipao again in bed. His hands roved over me, squeezing my breasts inside that embroidered silk, his head dipping into the valley of my cleavage. "My Chinese girl," he whispered, his breath hot against my skin. "My little empress."

I melted at his touch—even as I stared at a glass-encased qipao across the room and felt a tinge of unease, an inescapable flicker of warning.

Later, I wrote to my father back in Hong Kong. I told him about my new life in America, and the mansion I lived in. I told him I would wire him some money soon after I talked with my husband.

I told him I was very happy.

I began to notice Miguel more. He moved in his own world on the house grounds. Pruning the masses of azaleas, cleaning out the white marble fountains in the yard, washing down my husband's yacht. My husband also had a pontoon for use in the local waterways which he kept parked on a trailer in the street, and this became Miguel's new summer project, as it had been long neglected. He started with polishing the brightwork, then moved on to cleaning the spots of rust off its aluminum deck, spraying it down with Murphy's Oil Soap and scrubbing hard with a brush.

He never imposed, never came inside. A dog that knew its place.

So one day I took a glass of strawberry lemonade out to him.

He didn't see me coming down the driveway in my bare feet, so concentrated he was on his work. He glistened with sweat. It dripped from his brow, made his shirt cling to his body. His body was not like my husband's. My husband's, though not fat, was pale and somewhat slack. Miguel's was lean, bronzed, his muscles flexing hard and defined in the sun as he scrubbed away in his flip-flops.

He only looked up when he heard the electric gates open.

"Here." I offered the glass. "I thought you might be thirsty."

He did not smile, did not blink. Only bent down over the boat's rail to grab the sweating glass, our fingers brushing.

I went very still.

Then he had straightened and was swallowing the lemonade down in a greedy, unbroken bobbing of his Adam's apple before he sighed and wiped his mouth, handed it back. "Gracias, señora."

He grabbed his bottle of Murphy's Oil Soap, began to spray again.

"Why don't you take a break?" I suggested, almost blurting it out. "You've been out here a long time. And it's hot."

He shot a cagey sideways glance at Colding Mansion, his voice carefully flat. "Mr. Colding prefers I keep working until I finish the day's project."

"Oh." A strange heat crept up my neck. I glanced at the mansion's high foyer windows where the sun bounced off them in an angry glare, holding the empty lemonade glass and feeling unaccountably guilty.

But I did not go. I had a curiosity to satisfy.

"Well," I said, turning the glass in my hands. "You don't have to work while the lady of the house is talking with you."

He stopped spraying, cocked his head at me. For the first time, a smile spread across his face, lighting up his eyes, and I realized suddenly that he was very handsome.

"I suppose that's true," he said, wiping his hands with a rag and jumping down from the boat.

We stood in the shade while he tapped out a cigarette. He offered one.

I shook my head.

He sparked a lighter, the cigarette glowing in the shade as he pulled on it.

After he exhaled a cloud of smoke, I said with both vehemence and wonder, "I don't know how you do this. I hate cleaning things. I like mess, wildness, feeling free."

His lips twitched in a restrained smile as he took in my bare feet, the hair blowing about my face. "I can see that."

The blood flooded into my cheeks. To cover this, I shook the hair out of my eyes and cast about for a topic that would put me on firmer ground. "How long have you been working for my husband?"

He squinted, doing the calculations in his head. "Four years?"

"That's a long time."

He kicked at a rock. "Sí."

"How did you end up working for him?"

A change came over him at this question. He shifted, as if deciding on what to say, and ended up with grunting, "My family owed him."

He let the cryptic nature of that answer hang in the air.

There was a click and we both looked up to see the front door to Colding Mansion open. My husband stood on the stoop looking about.

Miguel quickly dropped his cigarette, stubbed it out with his flip-flop. "I should get back to work."

He started to pass me then, blocking my husband's view of me if he were looking this way. I thought he was going up into the boat. But then his hand shot out and seized my arm, so sudden and strong I didn't even have time to be scared, to let out a gasp of surprise. But that was not what stopped me. It was his face. The fierce intensity in it, lips parted as if groping for words.

He was going to tell me something.

But he didn't. He seemed to think better of it and released my arm, looking almost embarrassed. "Thank you for the conversation, señora," he said roughly and passed on by, climbing up into the boat.

My arm still throbbing from that grip, I looked past the gates and down the driveway to where my husband stood on the porch steps. Watching me.

THREE

"What did you two talk about?"

He waited only long enough for me to step inside so we were alone. His voice was light, almost aloof, but I felt myself tense.

"Nothing. The weather." I lifted the glass. "I brought him some lemonade."

He pulled the curtains closed, shutting out the golden haze outside, leaving us in darkness and shadow. "Are you so bored of me already?"

His voice was wounded, full of suspicion. It made me spin to him. "What? Of course not." I placed a hand on his chest. "You're my husband."

He searched my eyes, a great sadness in his face suddenly. It hurt my heart.

"That's right," he said at last, sighing as if coming to a decision, and kissed my forehead.

I woke the next morning to find him gone.

Foreboding gripped my heart in a cold fist. I slipped out of bed and padded out into the chilly marble of the house, calling his name. He was not there. Not in his study. Not on his yacht. Miguel was nowhere to be seen, and the Range Rover was gone.

I called my husband's phone, but it went straight to voicemail.

Just ran out for some errands, I told myself.

But why didn't he leave a note?

The hours passed, and when it became clear he was not coming back anytime soon, the panic began to set in. I hadn't been without him for a single day, a single afternoon, since I'd arrived at Colding Mansion, and I realized with shattering terror that I did not know who I was if he was not with me.

I paced the foyer, watching the gates and street, waiting to see the imposing SUV pull up. I chewed my nails bloody.

Where had he gone, and when would he be back? Had I done something wrong? Was this punishment for something?

Was this because I spoke to Miguel?

Eventually I crawled into bed, burning and writhing with misery, my stomach in knots. I felt as if I was taken with fever, as if I was purging something terrible from my body. Surely this pain had to end. Surely this must stop.

Desperate to distract myself, I wrote to my father. I told him everything was okay. That I was very happy.

At last, I fell into an exhausted sleep with the pen still in my hand, my pillow blotted dark with my tears.

I woke to the sound of the mansion gates opening.

My eyes flew wide. It was dark in the bedroom; night had fallen. But the sound had been real. I could still hear the whine of the electric gates.

I jolted upright, the sheets tangled in my legs, and staggered out of the bedroom, down the stairs, into the foyer where I yanked the front door open. I was met with the blast of the Range Rover's headlights blinding me like twin suns, along with it the sweet headiness of the bougainvillea, moist from a recent rain. A door clicked, and he stepped into the halo of those bright and terrible headlights, the shoulders of his coat beaded with shivering droplets, his mouth red in the dark. He looked more handsome than I had ever seen him.

I rushed down the drive in my bare feet and flung my arms around him, crying, pleading, the rain on his coat wet on my cheeks. "Where did you go?" I sobbed. "I didn't know where you went. I missed you. I missed you. Don't ever leave me like that again."

He waited until I subsided into ragged, hiccupping sobs, then drew me into his embrace, brushed my face with a gloved hand.

"I bought something for you."

I sniffed, pulling away to look at him. "You did?"

He was holding out a white box. He nudged it at me. "Open it."

I raised the lid with shaky fingers.

"Do you like it?"

I did not know what to think. I lifted it out of the folds of white tissue, my stomach heavy as lead.

It was a qipao.

"It's very beautiful," I whispered.

And it was. A rich red, swirling with gold designs. I knew I should be happy. Back home, I would have died for a qipao this lovely.

"I ordered it special for you," he purred above me. "I thought it'd look good on you." He placed a hand, very gently, on my shoulder. "Why don't you change into it."

I looked up at him, nodded. I was willing to do anything—anything—for him in that moment.

Not long after, he took me in our marital bed, ripping the new qipao in his passion. "My little empress," he whispered, over and over, as he moved above me.

That night, he tried new things. They were not preferable—not comfortable—but in my relief at his return I was not ready to admit to myself that I did not like them.

How can you not like love?

In the days that followed, my husband watched me around Miguel. But after that conversation in the street, the two of us did not speak again to each other beside the usual polite greeting. We both knew better.

I had begun to grow lonely. My husband's mood shifted after that night, and he spent more and more time in his study, on phone calls or drafting deals. Sometimes he had special guests over. They would play pai gow, mahjong, Chinese poker. He was a fiend for gambling. I asked him to teach me, hoping to share in his interests and get some of his attention I so craved. I did not care that I was terrible at it. All that was important was that we were spending time together.

And still. The loneliness and isolation grew, pushing roots deep inside me.

He began to grow irritable with me, and we had spats I had no appetite for. I didn't know what shifted, was desperate to get us back to those carefree early days. But it was no good. I had changed in his eyes. He had somehow lost respect for me, and I felt myself fallen off a pedestal, plunged into doubt and anxiety. I began to train myself to read his moods, to see the telltale sign of anger in his voice, the glint of suspicion in his eyes, as subtle as the shifts in fog. I became an expert at knowing when to make myself invisible or to fawn over him to soothe his temper. But it was never enough. I could never reach the perfection he demanded from me. There was always some fault to find, some flaw in my behavior. At first, I was plaintive, defiant, seeking his approval.

"What's happening?" I would ask. "Why are you like this?"

And his eyes would turn on me, dark and without feeling. "I don't really like your attitude right now," he would say, voice deathly quiet. "Do you really want to get into this?"

And the cold would seep into my bones.

One day, he had another business meeting in the foyer. I could hear him berating the suited associates in his loose shirt and shorts, the curse words slipping out as they did when he got angry. They took it all, cowed and attentive, willing to humiliate themselves to get his advice, his investments. I was not alone in this.

I shivered around the corner from the foyer, knowing he wanted me to come out again, parade myself in front of them. It was not only to manipulate things in his favor, I knew. It was a sign of status. Look at my beautiful wife. My exotic wife.

My trophy wife.

Outside, rain was falling, pummeling the windows, pounding the blooms of the bougainvilleas and azaleas. I did not want to go into that foyer. I couldn't. And I was equally terrified of what would happen if I didn't.

Then I saw Miguel.

He was out in the rain, under the pontoon on its trailer, blasting barnacles off its hull with a high-powered hose.

(Mr. Colding prefers I keep working until I finish the day's project.)

Disgust and outrage twisted my insides.

I used the side door to exit the house, splash down the driveway in my bare feet, my bare legs and shirt spotted with rain. I didn't care that my husband might see. I was too furious for that.

Miguel didn't notice the gates open, didn't notice me even when I was standing above him. The noise of the rain and hose were deafening. He'd blasted perhaps half the barnacles off, leaving lighter spots on the hull where they'd been, like removed scabs. Barnacle shrapnel was everywhere. Sharp bits and pieces all over Miguel, on the asphalt road he was lying on, cutting into his back through his white shirt. He was bleeding all over, traceries of faint red drifting out from under him in the rain.

A high-pressured spray got under the goggles he was wearing and he turned the hose off, lifted off the goggles and wiped at his eye, wincing.

That's when he saw me.

His hand froze, surprise and alarm furrowing his brow. "Señora." He cut his eyes at the house. "If Mr. Colding sees—"

"I don't care."

He frowned at me. Unsure, concerned, intrigued.

I held out a hand. "Get out from under there. This is ridiculous. I'm taking you inside."

Another glance at the house. "Señora—"

"I'm the wife of your employer," I shouted over the rain. "And I'm telling you to come inside."

His throat bobbed in a swallow. He took my hand.

I led him down the driveway into the side door. There was a bathroom there, mainly for the use of hired help, and I grabbed a stool and told him to sit on it. He did, looking both amused and afraid.

I shut the door, locked it, and put my wet hair up into a ponytail before opening the mirror, grabbing cotton balls and hydrogen peroxide. "Take your shirt off," I ordered.

He hesitated only a moment, then grabbed his soaked shirt clinging to his body and peeled it over his head, flinching as barnacles clicked onto the white-tiled floor. I couldn't help but stare. The cuts were all over, some of those hard-shelled crustaceans still embedded in his skin. And that skin was beautiful, powerful with muscles stacked orderly and smooth under that tanned flesh, like stones.

I became aware that he was watching me, something strange in his kind eyes, and I tore my gaze away, feeling a blush tingeing my ears red.

"I can't believe he made you stay out there like that," I muttered, going around him to start on his back.

When I pulled the first barnacle out, he did not hiss in pain, did not seem to feel it at all.

He shrugged as I tossed it into the sink. "I've had to do worse."

"Do I want to know?" I asked, plucking a barnacle out of his shoulder.

He snorted, dropping his head with a grin. "I don't think so, señora."

There was a small heap of barnacles in the sink now. That was the last of them. I unscrewed the cap on the hydrogen peroxide, poured some out onto a cotton ball and pressed it to one of the oozing wounds.

He did not flinch.

"Do you always tend to your hired help like this?" he asked, a smile in his voice.

"Seeing as how you're the only help I've ever had, I guess so." I inspected his back and, satisfied, grabbed a package of Band-Aids, began applying them.

"So no impertinent groundskeepers back in China, then?"

I let out a laugh. "Hardly. My father was a fisherman. We were—we were very poor. He thought I'd won the lottery when Mr. Colding proposed."

He turned his head, his voice low. "And what about you?"

I opened my mouth, shut it again. My hands, suddenly, were shaking. "I don't know anymore."

He nodded, his head turned to me, but not quite looking at me.

I swallowed and walked around him so we were face to face, eyed him up and down. "I think we're done."

But he did not seem to be listening to me. A look of concentrated wonder was pinching his brows. "I've never seen your hair up before."

My eyes flicked to his, then dropped. Something like self-consciousness, or anticipation, crawled over my skin. I shrugged a shoulder. "My husband likes it up."

"I like it down."

The sentence was so blunt, so honest, that my cheeks flared scarlet. Our eyes locked.

This was crossing a threshold, I knew. This was not proper.

I didn't care. Here, in this moment, I felt like a treasure.

Slowly, with trembling fingers, I reached up and undid the hair tie, let my hair fall wet and dark about my shoulders.

His eyes drank me in. I was shivering, the cold returning suddenly. I realized, with a thrill in my stomach, that my shirt was clinging to me, that my hardened nipples could be seen poking through the wet fabric, if he looked there.

He lifted a hand, his fingers twining in mine. The touch sent an electric charge through me.

I did not resist as he drew me forward until I was standing before him. My breath was shivering in and out between my lips, my arms twitching. Then his hands were on my hips, guiding me down onto his lap, my bare legs widening to straddle him. I could feel him pressed hard against me.

Desire settled, heavy and tingling, between my thighs.

He looked up into my face, his eyes going back and forth between mine. Rain still clung to his lips. They were very full, very close. I could see a fleck of barnacle clinging to his cheek. I wiped it away with a thumb, smoothed his slick black hair back from his brow. Then both my hands were on his face, and his hands were in my hair, tangling in it, angling my head back so his lips could press, very gently, to my throat.

Lust and foreboding coiled together in my stomach. I grinded, ever so gently, against him.

Then his hands were pulling my face down, and his lips were on mine with an almost ferocious tenderness. My nipples pinched. My toes curled. I felt myself getting wet.

Then I heard my husband's voice, raised in anger in the foyer, and I pushed myself off Miguel's lap in one explosive movement.

"I can't do this," I whispered, both hands raised as I backed away. My shoulders ridged up. Shame seared my insides. "I'm married. I can't—I can't—"

Miguel rose from the stool, his face pale. "I'm sorry, I didn't mean—"

"Get out." I unlocked the bathroom door and opened it, stepped aside.

He stood there a moment, as if considering saying more. Then he grabbed his shirt and slipped past me. We did not look at each other.

When I heard the side door click and shut out the pounding of the rain, I stood there staring at the bloody barnacles in the sink, not knowing what to feel.

When I stepped back into the main mansion, it was heavy with darkness, silent but for the rain tapping against the windows. The businessmen had left. The meeting was over.

All the tentative hope inside me shrank down to a small, trembling fear.

I made for the stairs, praying I could make it into the bedroom before he found me. Maybe he was in his study. Maybe he didn't know. Maybe—

My husband stepped out of the shadows at the foot of the stairs.

"Where were you?" he said in a low, deadly voice.

I came up short, my pulse beating madly in my throat. "Out—outside—"

"Outside," he said, taking in my wet clothes.

"Yes. I—I wanted to make sure your yacht was properly covered. I didn't want it to—"

It took him a single step to seize my jaw with one hand and squeeze hard, immobilizing me. I stared up at him with the wide, glassy eyes of frozen prey, my blood running cold.

He searched my face, checking for any signs of deception. Outside, lightning flared, throwing our shadows on the wall in a flash of white, and his face—in that sudden glare—was terrifying.

Slowly, his hand dropped away and he turned and started up the stairs into the gloom. "Change into your qipao," he called after me.

Afterward, still swollen and hard-used between the legs, I stared at the ancient qipao in its glass case on the far wall of the bedroom. Turned my head.

My husband's shoulder rose and fell in his sleep.

My jaw clenched.

Minutes later, I descended the stairs in the dark with all the qipaos he'd bought me in my arms. I dumped them into an empty marble fountain in the back yard, lit a match and watched the thousands of dollars of fabric blacken and burn, sending up a pillar of sparks and acrid smoke into the night. I waited, as still as the statuary of Colding Mansion, until those mandarin gowns were nothing but smoldering flakes of ash, as fluttery and fragile as duckfluff. And when their pulsing glow finally darkened, I swept the ashes into a dust pan and tipped them into the trash barrel by the side door, padded back upstairs and slipped into bed beside my still-sleeping husband.

I had never felt such satisfaction.

FOUR

Things changed after that night.

It was as if I'd thrown out all illusion along with the gifts he'd bought me, and I began to see him for what he was. Perhaps it was how alive I'd felt with Miguel. Perhaps that comparison finally revealed my husband's true nature to me. I had been making excuses for him, defending him in my head. But the patterns began to become clear, like a silhouette striding out of fog. His mysterious tests and silences that made me wonder what I'd done wrong, and which were only meant to distract me from his mistreatment and discourage me from holding him accountable. His playing the victim when he felt caught, so that I felt compelled to reassure him and give up addressing what had upset me in the first place. Bit by bit, that silhouette became clearer in my head, the face almost—almost—taking shape before me. The ever-shifting features of a devil.

This is how relationships end. People don't just drift apart without a little violence. There must be some slashing and clawing.

I no longer wrote to my father. I did not have the heart to tell him what my life had become, make him feel guilty about the marriage he had blessed. Or so I told myself. Because, of course, I was too ashamed to admit it. And I could not lie to him. Lord knew I had lied enough to myself.

And there was Miguel. How was I to walk about the grounds now, after what we had shared? How was I supposed to not feel guilty as I began to fantasize about him? About the way he looked at my hair? The taste of his lips on mine? His hands on me?

What I wanted him to do to me.

It only made me recoil now at my husband's touch. I made excuses to avoid his advances, saying I had a migraine, or that I was on my period, and he would look at me and say, "I don't mind a little blood."

I was terrified he would discover I'd thrown out the qipaos.

After another one of our spats, it got worse. This one had been more vicious, more cruel than the others, erupting during a game of mahjong. My valiant attempt to get through to him fell on deaf ears.

"I don't know why you won't take me out," I said, pleading for his explanation and understanding. "I don't have any friends here. I'm alone in this house. I can't wait around for you all day."

"No?" he said, and his eyes glittered—with offense, perhaps, or a feeling of betrayal. And he smirked and gave an apology that was not an apology, that was meant to make me feel crazy. "I'm sorry you feel that way."

This only infuriated me. I shook my head, disgusted, my voice rising despite myself. "I'm just another addition to your collection, aren't I?" I said, extending both arms to take in the antiquities all around us. "Your latest purchase from China." I laughed, reckless, knowing I was playing with fire, uncaring if I got burned. "You make me sick."

His eyes hooded, his face taking on a dangerous placidness, and dread pooled in my stomach.

"If that's what you really think," he said with lethal quiet, "why don't you fuck off back to that rathole in Kowloon I found you in?" He put a finger to his lips. "Oh, wait. You have no job and no money, don't you?"

My eyes filled with tears.

"I don't really like your attitude right now," he went on as he calmly placed a tile on the board, and I felt my muscles lock and become paralyzed under the familiar spell of those threatening words. "Don't ever talk to me like that again."

When I did not speak, he smacked the mahjong board off the table, sending it crashing against the wall in a clattering of tiles, snapping my eyes shut. "Yes?"

"Yes," I murmured, small and meek as a child.

I fled into the side yard where he couldn't see me, where the air was perfumed with the scent of bougainvilleas. Only there could I let myself break down. I could not show my feelings around him. He had no empathy, was uncaring of the torment he caused. On the contrary, his eyes glowed when he saw me in pain.

Because my reactions reminded him, after all, that he was alive.

When I felt the touch on my shoulder, saw Miguel's face close to mine, I did not question it. I turned into his arms and clung to him, sobbing. Here was truth. Here was something real.

Here was love.

"It's okay," he said, over and over. "You didn't do anything wrong, señora. You don't deserve this. You deserve better."

My heart ached and swelled. I nuzzled at him, and then my mouth was lifting, finding his. Our lips touched.

The drone of the bees filled the side yard.

"Take me away from him," I whispered, clutching him. "Take me away from all this."

He drew in a long, shuddering breath, as if he had been waiting, all along, for me to say this. "All right."

"When?"

"Soon," he said. "Soon."

My husband told me over breakfast.

"Our one-year anniversary is coming up."

I looked up from my plate of eggs and toast. He had been sickeningly sweet to me since our fight, pretending as if nothing had happened. But I had not expected him to remember our anniversary.

"Oh?"

"I thought we could make it our honeymoon trip. Take the yacht over to China." He gave me one of his most charming smiles. "What do you say?"

My mouth had gone dry, my mind a turmoil of thoughts. I poked at an egg yolk with my fork. "When?"

"Next weekend. The yacht needs to be prepared for the voyage first, naturally. I'll bring her over to my repair guy. We can pick her up Saturday night and take her over to the transport ship at Port Everglades."

I set my fork down, caught off guard by this ambush of kindness, the timing of it. I suddenly felt sick.

I gave him a beaming smile. "Sounds perfect."

"This Saturday?" Miguel whispered in the side yard, the hum of bees almost drowning out our voices.

"Saturday night." I leaned against the wall and tipped my head back, put a hand over my eyes. "He knows. He *knows*."

"Hey." He grabbed my hands. "It doesn't matter. We'll leave first, okay? I'll pick you up at seven."

"Seven," I mumbled.

"Hang in there. I just need to wrap some things up. Okay?"

"Okay."

Our kiss was a rushed and childlike thing, desperate in its intensity.

I spent that week in a dream. My husband would speak of our trip, the logistics of our flights, traveling to where lava met the sea. But I did not hear any of it. I was thinking of the life I would have with Miguel. I was thinking of freedom.

At first, it all felt like a dream, as fragile and untouchable as a mirage. But as the week went by, it took on shape and solidity. I could see Miguel and I in China with my father. I could see my husband giving in and signing divorce papers. I could see myself being happy again.

On Saturday, my husband left the house to wrap up some business affairs before our trip. "I'll be back around eight to pick you up," he said, placing a kiss on my brow. "See you soon."

I looked up into his eyes, forcing the edges of my lips up. "See you soon."

He touched my cheek, something unreadable in his face, and I held his gaze with all the innocence I could.

Then the corner of his mouth tugged in what was almost a smile, and he left.

As soon as the door shut, I began to pack.

I took only the clothes I'd brought with me to Colding Mansion—all save the qipao I'd worn on my first day at Colding Mansion, and in which I'd made love to my husband. I'd kept it when I'd thrown out all the ones he'd bought for me, hoping I'd have the heart to wear it again someday, that its association with home would return. That my love for my heritage would return.

But I knew that might be ruined forever.

I left the qipao on the hanger in my walk-in wardrobe.

At quarter to seven, I left my engagement ring on the conference table and walked out the gates of Colding Mansion to stand on the curb, my roller-bag at my side, my chest puffed up with excitement.

But seven o'clock came and went, and Miguel did not show.

I called him, but it went straight to voicemail. I sent him a text. *Where are you?*

I told myself he'd only been delayed. He'd be here at any moment, and the rest of my life would begin. I would leave all terror behind. I would know love again.

But the hour crawled on, and still he did not come.

At last, my lip began to tremble, and it sank in. The reality of it.

He was not coming.

I'd been stupid. Had I really thought this would work? Running off with the poor groundskeeper, changing my life, casting off the multimillionaire I'd married?

That didn't happen in real life. No. He'd gotten scared, perhaps been told off—bought off—by my husband, and decided not to show. He would find someone else, someone whose love was not so problematic.

I was alone.

I'd been an idiot.

I would always be married to that monster.

And Colding Mansion loomed behind me, taunting me with its opulence, its sickly cloying scent of azaleas and bougainvilleas, knowing I would return.

Tears filled my eyes. *So this is it*, I thought. *This is heartbreak.*

This is betrayal.

Then I saw the flash of sun glancing off tinted windows: a car was gliding down the street toward me.

My heart flew into my chest. My breath caught.

And the gleaming black Range Rover pulled up in front of me, the driver side window rolling down to reveal my husband's smiling face.

As we drove toward the marina, my husband kept glancing over at me.

I could not meet his gaze. I stared out the window, my stomach like lead, tears threatening the backs of my eyes.

"You excited?" he asked at last in a cheerful voice.

"Very," I murmured, seeing nothing but my reflection in the window.

There was silence for a minute as we drove. Then he asked another question, as delicate as commenting on the weather.

"Where's your ring?"

My stomach clenched.

"Oh," I said, staring blankly at my finger. "I must have forgot to put it back on after my shower."

"We can go back for it," he offered. "We have time."

"That's okay," I said, turning back to the window. "We shouldn't risk it."

He stared at me as we drove up to the marina gates, his eyes as black as stones.

It was sunset by the time we rolled our bags down the dock links, the sky flushed a violent pink above us. We'd parked the car by the office of the in-water yacht repair facility. Its windows were already dark, reflecting the sunset like the eyes of the possessed, but my husband said they'd left the keys on the boat for us. Everything was ready for departure.

It wasn't hard to find her. That bloody Sunseeker Predator was the only one in that corner of the marina.

My husband was brimming over with enthusiasm, sharing plans and ideas for the trip as he hopped onto the stern in his loose linen shirt and khaki shorts, his deck shoes. His dark, slicked-back hair ruffled slightly in the wind as he stowed his luggage, turned to grab mine.

It was the fish-and-garbage smell of the sea that brought it on, the lonely cry of gulls that made the fact of what I was leaving behind no longer avoidable. I could not hide from it. It all was bubbling up in me, the weight of what I'd lost. I began to tremble. Tears pushed into my eyes.

My husband's face fell. "Hey," he soothed, hopping onto the dock link to take my face in his hands. "What's wrong?"

I shook my head, helplessly, in his hands. I could barely get the words out. "I'm sorry, I—"

"Shh," he said, thumbing my tears away. "It's okay. I understand." His mouth twitched in sympathy, looking very red in the glare of sunset. He took his time, aiming for maximum effect. "Betrayal hurts, doesn't it?"

My whole body went cold.

"You're wondering why he didn't show, aren't you?"

I opened my mouth to protest, but he lifted a finger. "But he did show, my little empress. In fact, he's here with us right now." And he leaned to grab something hanging from the side of the yacht. Something black and shiny, braided like hair. He pulled hand over hand, drawing more of it out of the water with the flair of a magician. And then Miguel bobbed to the surface, the bloated skin of his face straining against the fishing net, cheeks bitten by the tiny mouths of fish, eyes rolled to the whites, lashes and hair crusted with salt.

"Should he come with us on the honeymoon?" my husband said, gesturing. "I'm sure there's room for the boy who wanted to fuck my wife."

A howling void opened within me.

The concrete of the dock hit my kneecaps. As if from very far away, I heard my own sobbing, felt my own hands reaching for that precious face. My Miguel.

But my husband let go, letting Miguel sink back into the water like a crab trap, and I shrieked—"*No!*"—before my husband slapped me down.

I stayed there, whimpering on all fours, my hair a black veil of mourning about me.

All was over. It was all over. Everything—everything—had been destroyed.

My husband stood over me, seething.

"You thought you could betray me? You thought you were better than me?" His fingers slid into my hair, tightened painfully, tilting my head back so I was forced to look up at him. His eyes were completely black, devoid of any pity. "You're *mine*," he whispered. "Forever."

And then, silky and low: "No more running, yes?"

My teeth clenched, my cheeks trembling in my fury. A version of me that had been suppressed for so long I'd forgotten who she was stirred and woke.

And meeting his eyes, I did not answer.

For the longest of moments, he did not react, his face going still in that way of his that did not let me know what he was thinking, that never failed to terrify me.

Then his nose thinned.

There was a crack as my head bounced off the concrete. Then his foot walloped into my stomach, driving all the air out of my lungs. For a small eternity, I could not suck in a breath. It was as if I had forgotten how to breathe altogether.

"This really what you want?" he hissed, and both his hands gripped, very tightly, around my throat. "I'll give you what you want."

And he began to squeeze.

I gasped, hands scrabbling at his thumbs pressing into my windpipe. Black spots danced in front of my eyes.

My husband's contorted face began to grow hazy, and I glimpsed behind him, very faint, the last light of the sun leak out of the sky. And a shadow blur past, quick and ragged as a bat.

So this was the end.

FIVE

When I opened my eyes again, I was coughing, gasping in huge lungfuls of air. The hands around my throat were gone. I pushed myself up onto one elbow, looking about.

My husband was there, not three paces from me. He was kneeling sideways on the dock link, an expression of utmost amazement on his face. And crouching over him was a shadow with its long white fangs buried in his throat.

All the hairs on the back of my neck stood on end.

With a sigh, the shadow dropped my husband to the dock. My husband did not move again.

The shadow rose to its feet.

It wore a dark suit, the darkness wrapping around it like a cape. Stars burned cold and clear in the sky behind it. As cold as its eyes.

"You are very lucky I chose this as my feeding ground tonight," the shadow said, unquestionably a man's voice. "If I hadn't had happened upon you . . ." He looked down at my husband.

I felt a chill.

The shadow looked back to me, his thick brows raised. "Are you coming?"

All the spit had dried in my mouth. It was painful to speak. "Wh—what?"

"It would seem you have left your old life behind you. And if you stay, you will be blamed for the disappearance of these men. If you come with me, no one will never find you."

Blamed. Disappearance. Never find me.

"I recommend you make a decision quickly."

I climbed unsteadily to my feet. My skull was pounding, my midriff throbbing with a dull, creaky pain. I wondered if a rib was broken.

"Come," the shadow said, and turned away.

As he passed my husband's body, he lifted a foot and pushed, sent the corpse sliding into the water with barely a ripple. As easy as that.

In my high, airy space of shock, this meant nothing to me. The shadow may as well have been playing with a ball.

A boat was waiting not far off. It was a long and gleaming thing, which I would later learn was a limousine tender. The shadow flowed down into it, turned to offer a hand.

But I hesitated, the suck of water around the dock pilings sounding eerie to my ears. A warning. "What are you?" I asked in a voice husky with terror, some old instinct returning.

"Nothing you need ever fear." The hand arched at the wrist, waiting.

I studied the shadow. He wore an almost bored look of forbearance, as if lying weren't worth his time. He was a man who simply took what he wanted.

I took his hand.

His skin was cold, terribly so. And he was very strong. In a moment I was down in the boat near the helm, and he was casting off, motoring us out into the bay.

I tried to collect my wits. All this was happening so fast, my brain was struggling to keep up. I glanced behind at the dock that was sliding away. I could still see the white gleam of my husband's yacht, and thought of the two men in my life sinking into the murk below the marina, forever entombed in my unconscious.

Swallowing, I turned back to the shadow that stood at the wheel, his dark, brambly hair gleaming in the starlight.

"Where are you taking me?" I asked, my voice not entirely steady.

The shadow's lips drew back in what I realized was a smile, and the starlight caught on his teeth, white and sharp. "To my home."

There was the shape of a boat out there, riding the dark swells. A yacht. It was long and sleek, with only its sidelights on, a thick rope tying it to a mooring ball.

The sight of it made me shiver.

"How did you get like this?" I whispered.

The shadow did not turn to me as he answered, his eyes fixed on the yacht. "Something like myself took me. Took my wife away from me. Now, I live to feed on the women who remind me of her, in hopes I will feel her love again."

I studied that pale face, struck by the blunt tragedy of its words. That was something I could understand.

"What's your name?"

The shadow glanced at me then, as if debating what secrets I deserved.

"You may call me Mr. Voper," he said, and turned away.

The yacht was huge now, blotting out the stars. The limo tender rounded its stern, and tall stainless-steel letters glinted on its transom: LAIR. Then that transom was opening like a hatch, revealing a pool lapping inside the yacht, and we were gliding into it, the water's wavering reflections dancing in pale blue patterns on the walls. Then the shadow called Mr. Voper was helping me out, guiding me through a dizzying maze of passageways. Suddenly, before me, a door was opened.

"This was the quarters of my former chief stew," he said. "You can sleep here tonight. And on the morrow, we will decide what to do with your life."

Then he was gone, gliding away down the hall toward a pair of double doors that glowed a deep red in the gloom.

I shut the door behind me, turned the lock. The bedsheets were cool against my skin. Comforting. I was too exhausted to cry, to even be overly fearful of my safety on this boat.

I slept.

When I woke, the red glare of early evening was filtering through the blinds. And I remembered the night before. Miguel. My husband. And that pale thing, that psychopath—Mr. Voper—drinking my husband's blood.

I stiffened, an old choking fear pushing against my throat. I bolted out of bed and swept out of the cabin, groped through the maze of hallways on the yacht. There. The way outside. I burst out onto the deck, and I saw that we were in some port full of a glitter of lights and waving palm trees. The passerelle. The gangplank-looking thing leading onto the dock. It was right there. I could escape.

I dashed to it, ready to flee into the night, run as far and as fast as I could from the creature that had brought me here.

But I halted, trembling, with my foot on the gridded wood, one hand on a stainless-steel stanchion, the breath rattling in my lungs.

It was absurd. I'd be a fool to stay here. I'd be a fool to stay with another man like Mr. Colding.

And yet, I hesitated.

"You're free to go, you know."

My heart jumped. A stewardess was standing behind me, looking inordinately calm. Her freckles shone on her cheeks in the glower of sunset.

"That's what he said. He wanted you to know that. He sleeps in the day, you see." She settled her shoulders, looking far too mature for her years. "But he'd like to dine with you tonight, if you wish."

I opened my mouth, not sure what I was going to say, but the stewardess didn't wait for me to reply. She simply slipped back into the yacht, leaving me alone on the deck.

I glanced out at the glittering harbor with its bristle of boat masts. Its crawl of traffic. The life it could promise me. And I felt a great emptiness.

After a while, I followed the stewardess back inside.

Mr. Voper did not eat a thing at dinner. He fingered the stem of a wine glass as he studied me across a long dining table overflowing with a phantasmagoria of roses. The glass was filled with something very red.

I ate but did not taste anything, my nostrils filled with the scent of those blooms. Mr. Voper, apparently, felt no need to break the silence, and eventually I became impatient. Why invite me if he wasn't going to speak with me?

But this was for me, I knew. This was for me to ask any questions I had.

And I did have them.

"Why?" I began.

He tilted his head, the wine glass stilling.

"Why did you save me? Why offer me a life here?"

He dropped his eyes, the edges of his mouth quirking as he turned the glass stem again. "Maybe because you also know what it is to lose everything."

I felt something in my chest contract. "And I'm just supposed to trust you? Even knowing what you are?"

His eyes flicked up at me. Very blue. Unwavering. "But you do trust me, don't you?"

I opened my mouth, shut it again. "Yes," I whispered. "I—I don't know why."

He nodded, looking somehow both sorrowful and amused. "I know why." He leaned forward, the tips of his fangs sliding out from under his upper lip. "Around me, you will never be in danger again."

The hairs on my arms pricked, and I felt a great settling in my guts. A hollowing out of all the knotted and sleepless worries stuck inside me.

I licked my lips. "And if I did decide to stay . . . what do you expect of me?"

He shrugged, leaning back in his chair. "Nothing you're not willing to do."

"Such as?"

He studied me from under his dark lashes, his mouth curving into something vaguely unsettling. "In time," he said, "you will come to see the importance of keeping things clean."

Of course, he meant cleaning up after the bodies.

I would see them disposed of. A procession of them, one after the other. Wrapped up in crinkly black garbage bags, dragged out of those red double doors of his master suite and tossed overboard into the water at night.

I would watch, and I would think of Miguel. I would think of my husband.

I would wonder why I was not running from this man.

One night, a buzzer woke me.

I sat up in bed, squinting in the dark. The buzzer was on the nightstand, its light blinking. Left over, no doubt, from the former chief stew. A means to summon her.

I tapped the buzzer off and slipped out of the bed and down the hall, as obedient as a child.

I did not question what I was doing. Nor did I tell myself it was out of a sense of curiosity, as I already knew where I was going and what would be waiting for me when I got there.

It all seemed so very normal and logical, as if I had been doing it all my life.

Those red double doors were slightly ajar now, glowing like blood. I put up a hand and creaked one wide.

The chamber was immense and as lurid as a womb, with soaring red canvases on the walls that looked like splashes of blood. And there *were* splashes of blood. On the bedsheets, the floor. There was the body of a blonde woman on the floor, her face drained of all color, her throat a great slash of crimson. And Mr. Voper was sitting naked on the edge of the bed beside her.

When he lifted his head and saw me in the doorway, he burst into tears.

"She's gone," he sobbed. "She's gone, and I can't get her back . . ."

My throat swelled shut. My eyes stung. And I knew, in that moment, what my life would look like.

"I know," I said, going to him. I sat on the bed beside him and drew him to me. "I know." He buried his face in my neck and I held him as he wept, letting him pour out his grief in a great wracking of his shoulders, as patient as a housewife. For that is what I would be, I knew. A housekeeper, a housewife to this monster—a replacement for his lost wife, in all ways but romantic.

Yes. This is the life I would be signing up for. I could not trust anyone after Mr. Colding, after all. I was choosing now a Mr. Colding whose abuse was at least dependable, understandable. I would know how to please this man, unlike Mr. Colding. Let him fuck and suck, and I would clean up the mess, tend to his grief, be his accomplice.

I looked down at my feet, where that blonde was lying on the floor in her pool of blood. For a moment, it was no longer her. It was Miguel.

Yes. That was okay. At least I would have some purpose this way. I could live with that. We could grieve together.

This is how I would survive.

In the morning, I put on a yachtie skirt and shirt, fitted tight and forbidding. Then I looked at my hair in the mirror, long and dark and tumbling free about my shoulders.

When I stepped out at dawn onto the aft main deck, the stewardesses were waiting for me in a nervous line. They wore skirts and polos, like myself. And like myself, they wore their hair up in tight, severe buns.

I clasped my hands before me and looked about at them all, sweeping them with an imperious gaze. "Hello ladies," I said. "I am Mrs. Colding."

With the passing of the years, I grew more and more accustomed to my role. One could say I took it too far. But no one could deny that I excelled at it. Eventually, I forbade anyone else from entering Voper's suite, and our friendship took on deep and strange roots, the number of crewmates knowing Voper well shrinking to just myself. I told myself I did not trust anyone else to attend to his needs. This was how I did not face how much I depended on him.

One night, I was scrubbing blood off the tiles of his ensuite head when I felt it come over me. An immense calm. A containing of things, followed by a blinding relief that left me on all fours, shivering and hands spread on the cool tiles, as if afraid I would be sucked up into the sky.

I took over the disposing of the bodies after that.

Before I knew it, I had come to love cleaning, the orderliness of things. The erasure of what came before.

In the back of my mind, there was the uneasy suspicion that I had begun to resemble Mr. Voper in more ways than were good for me. Once in a while, I would catch him watching me, and know what he was thinking. That, like him, I had taken on a nature that sought to control things that could not be controlled.

I never once took a lover, because I knew I wouldn't trust them. That it would never last, never mean anything.

Never replace anything.

I grew to revel in my solitude. It became my strength.

Or so I told myself.

Mr. Voper sighed as he studied me in my quarters. "I already got rid of the purser for you—"

I waved a hand. "Couldn't trust that girl. It's more efficient to have me do it myself. Now this captain—"

"About that—"

"I really don't know how I am supposed to perform to the best of my abilities with that man. How can I provide you what you need when the captain won't pick up a radio and communicate with me? If the captain won't inform me when the guests are returning to the boat, I can't have dinner ready at the appropriate time, now can I?"

"Mrs. Colding—"

"I also need a say in the hiring of the crew. These babes in the woods this captain keeps sending me simply won't do."

"*Mrs. Colding.*"

"What?" I snap, looking up from my tablet. "What?"

"I know," Mr. Voper said, a slight smile curling his lips. "That's why I hired a new captain for you. He starts immediately." And he inclined his head, indicating behind me.

My stomach dropped. I turned, and there was a tall, broad-shouldered shadow in the doorway.

"I hope he's up to your standards," Mr. Voper finished.

The shadow stepped forward, and my heart jammed in my throat. It couldn't be. Not him. Not my husband. He was gone. He was—

And a man in a captain's epauletted polo stepped into the light.

Relief rolled through me.

The man looked a few years older than me, in his mid-fifties. Still muscular for a man his age, his hair a dashing wave of silver, his eyes the gray of sea mist.

And he had heard my entire rant.

My neck flushed a deep red, and then we locked eyes.

It was like a spark. The jolt of an electric charge, as undeniable as the sun.

But I tried to deny it anyway.

I lifted my nose, my icy aloofness intact again, and held out a hand. "Mrs. Colding. The chief stew."

The man smirked at this, throwing Adrian a sideways glance, and took it. "Mr. Redfearn. The new and apparently very short-lived captain."

The handshake lingered. His hand was warm, rough, with the thick calluses of a man who had spent all his life at sea. I knew I should let go. But I didn't.

That touch was causing sparks and chills all over my body, in a way I never thought I'd feel again. I didn't want it to end.

"Short-lived?" I said at last, and raised a considering eyebrow. "Perhaps. Perhaps not."

And we stared at each other, this new shared thing held between us, as a rakish grin curled up the side of Captain Redfearn's mouth, promising everything.

PART TWO:

THE OPEN SEA

SIX

It is as if all air and sound has been sucked out of the world.

I cannot hear. A high-pitched whine fills my ears, blocking out the crackle of the flames burning on the South China Sea. They lick the night in a silent dance, as if in celebration of the demise of Castle Volok. Sparks drift through the air like fireflies. Heat blurs and warps everything, turning the apparition of the yacht approaching us into a demonic dream.

And all I can see is that other apparition at the bow of that boat.

All I can see is him.

Captain Redfearn's face moves in front of me. His mouth is moving. He is saying something, grabbing me by the shoulders, shaking me. I cannot hear him. All I can do is blink at him, try to speak into that soundless void. I can, to my amazement, hear what I say, the words rising up as if from great muffled depths, shattering the world as if it were made of glass.

"It's my ex-husband," I gasp. "It's Mr. Colding."

And it's as if saying it aloud makes this dream finally real. All the little hairs stand on my arms. My stomach bottoms out. My mouth dries. He's back. Somehow, somehow, he survived. And he came back for me. He's clawed his way back from death to claim me. To make me his again.

I can't breathe. I heave in air in long, wheezing draws, but I can't get enough in my lungs. I reach out with dumb, shaky hands like a woman in the throes of an asthma attack. I'm trembling all over, hot with pins and needles in the wetsuit I wore to rescue Redfearn. My knees buckle and I sink into the floor of the tender boat, my back to the helm station.

"Hey." Redfearn kneels in front of me, eyebrows pinched. "Hey, it's okay—"

I clutch onto him with desperate strength, lock my eyes onto his. "Don't."

"What?"

"*Don't*," I gasp. "Don't let him take me."

Redfearn's face slackens. Then fills again with cold, hard rage.

He turns, sweeping up the yacht controller, and mashes a button with his thumb.

The blast from the sound cannon at the bow of the *Thing* is excruciating, even with that yacht being beside us, keeping us safe outside of the cannon's range. I can *see* the effect of the blast. It whirls the airborne sparks away like snowflakes in a blizzard. The flames on the sea flatten. The sea itself trembles and feathers with ripples, shooting a path straight toward the Steward's yacht.

And I see him. He ducks his head with a curse, hands over ears, and then that yacht that looks like a high-tech Chinese junk is veering away, its red sails luffing and snapping in the wind.

Giving us the time we need to get away.

In a moment Redfearn is at the helm, the yacht controller hanging from its yellow lanyard about his neck, and the world swerves and blurs into streaks of orange light as he brings us about, slingshotting us toward the stern of the *Thing*. He must have pressed the yacht controller again, because the boat's anchor lifts out of the sea as we pass it, its iron flukes dripping water.

I shut my eyes to stem the nausea, one hand held to my stomach. I can feel the sweat spring out all over my body, as if I've been taken with fever.

But that doesn't blot away that image of my husband. My abuser. My nightmare.

That stays with me.

The whine of the tender's twin diesel engines lowers and dies, and then Redfearn's hands are under my armpits, pulling me up. "Come on."

We're there. Redfearn is leading me like a child still half-asleep, still in the grip of a bad dream. We hop onto the swim deck, not bothering to stow the tender. I manage to make it up the teak stairs onto the aft main deck before my knees fail again, and Redfearn sits me down onto a banquette along the *Thing*'s starboard side.

Then Redfearn is gripping the yacht controller and working its joysticks, yawing our bow about to get us going. The thrusters hum beneath us, setting the water at the stern into a churning froth that whirls the tender away.

And the world spins like a sickening carousel again, revealing the Steward's yacht has fallen in line behind us, once more in pursuit. The Steward at its bow.

That's when we hear it.

"Dad?"

Redfearn and me whirl about. We had thought the boat abandoned. It *should* be abandoned, its crew left behind in Macau. But there's a form stepping out of the shadows of the yacht's interior. It's barefoot, in a ghostly white nightdress, blonde hair hanging in matted tangles about its face. Tears tremble in its eyes.

It's Penelope.

She must have finally woken from her uncanny slumber. Must have stowed away on the yacht when Redfearn set out to offer himself to the Steward in sacrifice for her life. And without Redfearn knowing.

At least, if Redfearn's face is anything to judge by.

I turn to look at him. His muscles have slackened, his lips parted. His gray eyes glass up as he looks on his daughter. "My little sun," he whispers.

And then Penelope is running to him, and Redfearn is opening his arms, half-sobbing in joy.

But Penelope does not run into his embrace. She is caught awkwardly in Redfearn's left arm as she tries to run past him, and then he is holding her back in stunned confusion as she screams and weeps, one hand reaching desperately beyond him.

Beyond him, toward the yacht behind us.

Beyond him, toward the Steward.

"Pen?" Redfearn says, his voice cracked in heartbreak.

But she does not look at her father.

"No!" she shrieks, straining and weeping in her grief. "Let me get back to him! Please! *My love! My love!*"

And Redfearn and I stare at each other, tipped into horror.

SEVEN

Redfearn's daughter cries and pleads, the tears pluming at the corners of her eyes and spilling down her face. "No! *No!*" she wails, her voice raw with anguish. Then her hands are pounding on Redfearn's chest in futile fury and she suddenly surrenders, sagging in his arms as she dissolves into a fit of weeping.

And the Steward watches from the bow of his yacht. Even from here, even across that distance, I can see it. His smirk of twisted and gloating pleasure.

A hard, vengeful anger forms in the pit of my stomach.

When I look back at Redfearn, he is staring over his daughter at me with imploring eyes. "Please," he whispers, glancing at the top of Penelope's head and then away, his lip trembling. "I can't." He hooks a chin toward the Steward's boat. "I have to—"

I nod. I understand.

My legs are steadier than I thought they'd be. I wipe at my eyes and take Penelope by the shoulders, gently pry her away from her father. "Come," I say in my calm chief stewardess voice. "Let's get you inside."

As I steer her down the length of the main deck's infinity pool toward the yacht's interior, I glance back at Redfearn. He's wiping a hand down his face, working his jaw as if that will reset things, keep the grief and despair he wants to give into at bay. Then he lifts the yacht controller from his chest and faces the Steward.

That's the last I see of him as I guide his daughter inside.

I take her to one of the VIP guest suites. She's quiet now, drained and leaning into me by the time we step inside, and she immediately crawls into bed and curls into a ball.

I do not know what to do. I am on edge, nervy with adrenaline and shock, and not a small amount of apprehension.

I need to be careful here.

I sit straight-backed on the edge of a chair by the bed, feeling ridiculous and out of place in my wetsuit in this lavish suite. I fold my hands in my lap.

"Penelope?"

The ball of misery on the bed does not answer.

I swallow. "My name is . . ." I trail off, think better of it, and try again. "I've heard a lot about you over the years. I'm happy to finally meet you."

She does not seem to hear me. She hugs herself, shivering as if taken with cold, slowly writhing on the bed like someone suffering through withdrawal.

"Is there anything I can do for you?"

She squirms and writhes, glistening with sweat. The whisper that comes back to me is pitiful, tear-choked, almost sensual: "Take me back to him."

I go cold all over.

I look down into my lap, at my fingers twisting there. "You mean the Steward."

Her head moves in a nod on the bed.

"Is he—is he your lover?"

Another nod.

An uncontrollable wave of disgust and horror rises up in me, and it's in this moment that I notice, through the shifting tangles of her golden hair, a pair of fang marks on the curve of her neck where it meets her shoulder.

My insides turn over. I have to shut my eyes, bite the inside of my lip, to ride out the overwhelming roll of nausea.

After a long, steadying breath, I open my eyes again. "You know what he is, then."

"So?"

"You know he feeds on women. That he had boatloads of them shipped to his castle so he could—"

"Shut up!" she snarls, turning her head to not quite look at me.

I lean forward, filling my voice with urgency and concern. "You can't ignore that, Penelope. He's an abuser. He uses people—"

"You don't know anything!" She pushes herself up from the bed to glare at me, and I tense. She is fiercely beautiful, almost carnal in her position, heated with unfulfilled longing. Then her shining face softens into that of a child's. "He's kind. He's sweet to me—"

I think of his cajoling charm in the innocent early days of our marriage, him turning it on this young woman—laying his hands on her, his teeth—and feel sick. "He's always like that in the beginning, dear—"

"You don't know him," she snaps, mulish again. "You don't know anything."

I slowly shake my head, barely managing to hold back a scoff. "Oh, I know him—"

"Really?" Her jaw juts out in scornful defiance as she eyes me up and down. "And how would an old woman like you know?"

I open my mouth, hesitate—

And Penelope Redfearn lies back down on the bed, shivering again. "You can fuck off now."

Before I find Redfearn, I go to my quarters, quickly shuck off my wetsuit, rinse off in the shower and change into my stewardess clothes, pin up my hair into its bun. The relief of being clean again is so pure, so immense, I feel as if I am rinsing off more than the sweaty, salty grime of my recent exertions. There is another, stickier grime I am rinsing away.

Whatever I had thought Penelope would be like, it was not this. But I know I did not see the real Penelope in that suite. That poor girl was the lovestruck shell of someone parted from their abuser.

My abuser.

Of course. Not only was he back—horrifyingly, nightmarishly, irrefutably—but he's seduced the daughter of the one I love. I could almost laugh at the twisted comedy of it.

This was inevitable. This was always meant to be. He is like my curse, always finding a way to worm himself back into my life, trying to take everything from me.

A part of me—a dark, cruel part of me that speaks with his voice—tells me that this is my fault. That I am responsible for this.

I push this back into a far corner of my mind, somewhere I promise myself I will never look again. I have other things to attend to.

Because now, I know, I have to protect her.

I have to save her from what I went through.

I stop by the galley, bring a plate of meat and cheese and a glass of water to Penelope's room. "In case you're hungry," I say gently, and set them on the nightstand.

But Penelope does not hear. She writhes on the bed with her back to me, her hands hugging herself, roving over herself, feeling her skin marked by the fangs of her lover, and it seems—I can barely watch—that her hips grind against the sheets.

No. That's not what she's hungry for.

A queasy revulsion works its way down my body as I slip out of the room.

Redfearn is not on the aft main deck. But the Steward's yacht is still behind us, a dark shadow with its jagged red sails lit by uplights. There's perhaps three miles of distance between us now, and I can no longer see the Steward at the bow, no longer see the fiery grave of Volok's castle flickering in the night. We are in the middle of nowhere, bounded by darkness.

And as I watch, I can tell—though it's almost imperceptible—that the Steward's boat is gaining on us.

A chill touches the back of my neck.

I find Redfearn in the wheelhouse. I stare at him a moment through the window of the heavy sliding door before I pull it back. He leans with both hands on the flat panels of the bridge controls, the light from the black box units making his face glow. He's set the yacht controller aside, set the *Thing*'s course on autopilot and stares straight ahead like a man lost in old regrets, old pain.

Sympathy twists at me, and I touch the half-moon pendant hanging from my neck. The necklace he gave me in the hotel room in Macau, before he vanished to sacrifice himself for his daughter. *My sailor moon*, he called me. The light in his world that always showed him out of the dark.

I have to be that light for him now.

I haul on the door.

Redfearn glances over at me as I slip inside, gives me a wan smile. "Hey."

"Hey."

He can keep it together for only a moment. Then the muscles at the corners of his jaws bunch and he takes in the sharp kind of breath that holds in a sob.

I go to him, wrapping my arms around him. "I'm so sorry," I whisper.

His nod brushes my hair, his arms tightening around me. "Thanks," he croaks. And then, almost as if he's afraid to ask: "How's she doing?"

I pull back to look at him. "She's hanging in there. She's . . . in a lot of pain."

His eyes glass up and he nods again, his eyes darting away. He works his throat. "Is she . . . angry?"

I don't want to say it. But I have to. "Yes."

His mouth twitches. His lips purse together as he turns away, leans again on the blinking panels. "And she's . . . she's really . . ."

"She is," I say, assuming my chief stewardess voice: time to rip off the Band-Aid. "She's completely under his control. He does this. It's the way he manipulates people. He gets inside your head, makes you dependent on him. Creates a trauma bond. There may be some kind of vampire magic mixed up in this, too. I don't know. Her body addicted to his feeding."

He goes rigid, his voice low. "Addicted?"

This is the worst part, I know, and I don't know how he'll react. I find myself tensing. "I think she's . . . going through withdrawal. It seemed . . . sexual."

Redfearn's eyes squinch shut, a low huff of breath coming out of him. His hands curl into fists on the panels. He practically vibrates with rage.

But there's more to it than that.

"Hey," I tell him, laying a hand on his back and rubbing in tiny circles. "She didn't get that from you."

"Like father like daughter," he laughs before choking it back.

"*No*." I shake my head. "You didn't pass that strain in your family down. This addiction—it's not natural."

"Maybe not," he gruffs, pushing himself upright again as if to face a fact head on. "But I drove her to it."

I clasp my hands in front of me. "Maybe. But you also saved her from it. You got her back. You can still make things right."

He looks at me, appreciation gentling his face. "Yes. After I take care of our current problem." His eyes grow sad, tender, as he takes hold of my arms. "You okay?"

I feel my sense of stability wobble. A muscle twitches in my face, making my eyelid flutter. I clear my throat. "Mmhmm."

"I'm sorry I couldn't stay with you—"

"I understand," I say quickly, tilting my chin at the yacht controller. "You had to—I get it."

He stares intently into my eyes. "You thought he was gone."

I jerk my head in a nod, breathe in hard through my nose. "When Adrian bit him, he must have gone too far and turned him. And now . . ." I meet his eyes, my voice growing small. "I feel like I'm coming undone, Redfearn."

He's taking me in his arms now, wrapping me up in his warm, comforting bulk. "I won't let him do anything to you. *Anything.*"

I clutch onto him, shut my eyes as I lay my cheek against his chest. "What are we going to do?"

His voice rumbles into my ear. "I was an idiot and got rid of the rocket launcher when we docked in Macau. And this guy"—he reaches behind his back and lifts out the Glock he brought with him to Castle Volok, clicks it down on a flat panel display—"is out of ammo. So we don't have any weapons besides the sound cannon. And we're running low on fuel." He taps the glowing red fuel gauge with its drooping needle. "Sooner or later, he's going to catch up to us. And when he boards us . . ."

We both grow quiet, knowing what would happen then.

"I need time to think and come up with a plan." Redfearn sighs, deep and somewhat irritated with himself. "For now, we have to find a place to hide."

"Where?" I scoff, glancing out the windows at the trackless night around us. "We're on the open sea."

"There might be a place," Redfearn says, moving to a chart table behind the helm station where a faded blue nautical chart is laid out. It's one of the charts Redfearn kept from his time as captain on the *Lair*, annotated with his crude chicken scratches. A map of the southern coast of China. "If I'm right, it should be near us. We might even be able to siphon fuel into our tanks there."

"What is it?" I say, drawing close to peer at the chart.

"It's an old place few know about." His finger trails from an X marked CASTLE VOLOK to another X farther out to sea. "It's where they dump their yachts when they're done with them. Get rid of evidence."

And his finger taps on the chart.

I squint, a chilly foreboding settling in me. The place is called—

PART THREE:

THE GRAVEYARD OF LAIRS

EIGHT

I check again on Penelope, and relief washes through me when I find she's fallen into an exhausted sleep.

Best she's not awake for what's next.

When I step out onto the portside gangway and look astern, I can see her—the boat of our pursuer, its jagged dragon wing sails glowing. She's gained perhaps a half mile on us.

A shudder works its way down my body.

There are footsteps behind me, and I turn to see Redfearn, the yacht controller hanging from his neck, a crew radio in hand. "Ready?" he asks.

I nod.

He opens the aft deck storage locker and dips inside to open the boat switch panel. For my part, I make my way down into the lower deck, through the saloon with the glass bottom of the infinity pool overhead, to the tender garage at the stern. I place my hand on a switch on the wall, unclip my crew radio from my hip. "You can kill the lights down here." After a moment, the few lights flick off, leaving me in darkness. Then I flip the switch. The hatch whines up, revealing a rectangle of star-dusted night, those glowing red sails in the distance. That boat is even closer now.

But I'm not concentrating on that. I only have eyes for the Jet Skis stored on chocks on either side of the tender garage.

Another switch, and one line of metal chocks extend out over the swim deck on wheels. I unhook the straps securing the aftmost Jet Ski to the chocks, thumb my crew radio again. "Ready?"

"Ready."

I take a breath. "Now."

I turn the sidelights of the Jet Ski on. At the same time, all the lights on the *Thing* go dark. She is a ghost at sea.

And I push the Jet Ski out into the water, leaving her drifting behind us, her red and green side lights bobbing on the dark sea.

The stern thrusters are kicking in, turning the *Thing* so she's diverging from the decoy, as the tender garage whines shut behind me.

I have to use my phone light to navigate my way back through the benighted innards of the boat. I tap it off before stepping out onto the main deck gangway again to rejoin Captain Redfearn.

Together, we stand—two shadows on a dark ship—as we watch the lights of the Jet Ski and the Steward's boat.

We don't know if it will work. Don't know if the radar of that boat will pick us up. But the distance for most pleasure vessel radars is only a mile. We're beyond that.

And as the *Thing* continues on into the dark away from those sets of lights, we wait, hands white-knuckling the rail.

If the Steward knows he's been tricked, he'll be diverting course at any moment to follow us. Any moment.

Now.

But that Chinese junk doesn't. It continues on after the Jet Ski. The decoy has worked.

We let out a breath we didn't know we were holding.

"We only have a minute or two before he discovers the ruse." Redfearn can't help but grin in the dark. "Let's make the most of it."

We ramp the *Thing* up to its maximum speed, her bow cutting through the waves in white leaps of spray. We stand by the sound cannon, eyes peering into the dark. It should only be a few minutes before we arrive at our destination, if it in fact exists.

We are under no illusion that the Steward will know where we've gone, once he finds the Jet Ski. Our hope is that we'll at least buy ourselves enough time to hide.

And soon enough, I see what we'll be hiding in.

The cloud wrack that had been obscuring a glowing full moon parts, and I see, far off, the gleam of moonlight on metal.

Redfearn and I step closer, placing our hands on the rail at the bow. And I lift a pair of binoculars to my eyes to get my first glimpse of the Graveyard of Lairs.

The flesh creeps along the back of my neck.

It's an atoll. A ring-shaped coral island encircling a lagoon. I can make out the delicate white gleam of sand in the moonlight, a round reef formation with a diameter of perhaps twenty kilometers. And in its central lagoon are heaped the ghostly wrecks of hundreds of superyachts.

"My God," I breathe, lowering the binoculars.

As we draw closer, cruising alongside the atoll's ring, I see that these yachts are of every size, every make. A gathering of unnerving silhouettes in that tropical gloom. Some grand and new, some ancient and deteriorated, tilting drunkenly in their lagoon grave like tombstones. The abandoned homes of centuries of vampires, rusting away in eerie silence.

"Fuck."

I tear my eyes away to follow Redfearn's gaze, and my blood chills. The lights of the Jet Ski have drifted far off over the sea. And the Steward's yacht is bearing down on us, no more than two miles off.

"We need to find a way inside," Redfearn growls.

He amps up the speed on the *Thing*, our eyes trained on the atoll as we round it. Its ring of sand is perhaps three meters tall, five meters wide. And seemingly endless.

I glance behind again. The Steward's boat is perhaps a mile out now. It'll be on us in less than a minute.

I think of his face, his smirk of triumph as he hops aboard the *Thing* to claim me and Penelope, and a catalyzing terror grips me.

There's no need for secrecy any longer, so I man a searchlight at the bow, blast it on and aim it along the shoreline.

And we find it.

It's a break in the atoll of maybe the width of three boats, its horns of sand curving inward, the color of the water changing in a swirl of silt as it enters the lagoon.

When Redfearn guides us in, I throw a look over my shoulder, my heart pounding. But we've lost sight of the Steward's boat. She's on the far side of the atoll now.

No knowing how far, how close.

We have to hide. Now.

And I turn back to the searchlight and train it on the Graveyard of Lairs.

It seems to jump out at us, a rearing up of ghost ships crowding close like cold and gruesome corpses in the white blast of the searchlight. Redfearn slows the *Thing* down to a crawl as we thread our way through the graveyard, skirting its dangers: The vast hulks of megayachts mottled red with oxidization, still with fenders hung over their sides. The drooping lines of anchor chains, stiff with rust and dripping flags of seaweed. Ancient schooners with splintered and leaning masts, ragged sails flapping spookily in the wind. Under the glare of the searchlight, the names of boats gleam on transoms, some pitted and disfigured by the slow corrosion of salt: REVENANT, PHANTOM MAID, FLYING BLOODMAN.

Redfearn takes us deeper and deeper into the atoll's maze, until he lifts a finger. "There."

I train the searchlight on where he's pointing: a narrow space between two yachts bigger than ours. Just wide enough to fit us.

And glancing behind, I see another searchlight. A white beam sweeping through the graveyard and over yacht signs, hunting for us.

But they haven't seen us yet.

"I need to do something," I tell Redfearn, starting for the stern.

The captain grunts as he throws a fender over the side, one eye on the *Thing*'s prow easing in between the boats. "Go. I got this."

I pad down the gangway, dip into the storage locker and grab two toolboxes: an electric drill and a ratchet wrench set. Then down into the tender garage again, listening to the whine of the door open. As the *Thing* glides into her hiding spot, I step out onto her swim deck, peer back where we came.

That other searchlight sweeps the rotting hulks of yachts like the beam of a lighthouse. Closer.

So I get to work.

I take out the drill, unscrew an access panel on the inside of the garage door above me, revealing a mass of LED wiring and fiber optic cables feeding into the illuminating steel letters on the outside. And the screws mounting the letters in place, fastened tight with nuts.

I grab the ratchet wrench and begin on the nuts.

By the time I'm done, clicking the toolboxes shut, the Steward's boat is rounding the corner into the aisle of boats we're in, red sails glowing lurid and demonic. Its searchlight turns like a blazing eye toward me.

Blood pounding, I dive inside with the toolboxes, slap the switch to close the tender garage door.

When I dash up onto the gangway again, my heart in my throat, Redfearn is standing there in the dark like a man awaiting the gallows.

He places a finger to his lips.

And when I turn, skin crawling, the Steward's boat glides into view.

Up close, she looks like a vision, a relic out of time. Her shallow hull may be black-painted steel, but she has a sternpost rudder and a high poop deck and bulwarks crafted from blackened teak and fir timber filigreed in red, glowing Chinese lanterns strung along her upper deck. She floats upon the dark waters like a burning phantom, her deck uplights spotlighting her jagged fans of red sails and giving them the illusion that they're on fire. A mythic and predatory thing, out for blood.

And standing at her bow, the Steward—my ex-husband, my abuser—mans the searchlight like a wrathful god.

My insides freeze. My scalp constricts.

And he lifts his bullhorn to his lips.

"Still running, I see."

His voice blasts out into the silence of the graveyard. Knowing. Contemptuous. Insinuating itself inside my head, deep into the folds of my brain, awakening those old synapses of panic and despair.

"You thought you could get away last time. What makes you think now will be any different?"

He's right, I know. I've been a fool, haven't I?

He's going to find me. He's going to take me again.

He's going to claim me as his bride once more.

"You will always be mine," he purrs.

At my side, Redfearn glances at me, slips his hand into mine and squeezes.

The searchlight roams over the boats across from us, lingering on the stainless-steel letters of their signs.

"You will always be Mrs. Colding."

And then the Steward is swinging the searchlight about on its pole in a powerful sweep of light, blazing it right at us.

Redfearn grabs me, ducks us both into an alcove in the *Thing*'s superstructure as the beam flashes down the gangway, just missing us.

And then it's gone.

"Can you hear me, Penelope? Are you awake, my sweet?"

Redfearn's eyes, inches from mine, widen in rage.

And we hear it: a door sliding back on its tracks. Penelope steps out onto the gangway in front of us, her bare feet shuffling like a sleepwalker's, the beam's light shining through her white nightdress as it sweeps close, terribly close, giving her the appearance of an angel.

"If you can hear me, call to me. Tell me where you are."

And Penelope's body stiffens, as if waking from an enchantment.

She lifts her arms—

And Redfearn dives for her, reaching around her to clamp his hand over her mouth, drag her down onto the deck as the searchlight sweeps past overhead.

I duck back into the alcove, a hand clamped over my own mouth, holding back a sob.

"Don't worry. I promise you: They won't keep us apart. I'll come for you. I love you."

I hate you, husband. I hate you.

And I can see, in the reflection in the deck-to-ceiling windows of the boat beside us, that the searchlight is lingering on the name of our boat.

Dread presses down on me. Will it work? Will I really outsmart him here, when he managed to outsmart death itself to come back for me?

And then the searchlight sweeps on.

That Chinese rig glides like a specter of death into the labyrinth of the graveyard, and the bullhorn echoes back to us, floating on the cool night air.

"You can't hide forever in here. Day will come, and I will find you." I can hear the smile in his voice. "Sweet dreams, my sweet. Sweet dreams, little empress."

And those glowering fan sails disappear into the gloom, leaving the graveyard silent, the brightwork of its ships gleaming coldly in the moonlight.

Lowering the hand from my mouth, I let out a long, wavering breath through rounded lips and step out onto the gangway, afraid of what I'll see.

Redfearn cradles his daughter in his arms. She seems to have fainted in her hysteria, and he brushes her hair with a hand, his lip quivering in helpless rage.

I hold a hand to my stomach. "Redfearn?"

When he looks up at me, tears stand in his eyes.

He lays his daughter down with great tenderness, descends the teak stairs onto the swim deck to stare after the Steward's boat, make sure it's really gone.

"How?" he says, the word a throaty growl. "The light was right on—"

And he sees the name on the transom, and what I'd done to it: rearranging those stainless-steel letters from THING into NIGHT.

He looks up at me, standing at the head of the stairs on the aft main deck. His mouth twitches in a smile despite himself.

"You're a genius, Mrs. Colding."

And he strides up the stairs into my arms. The two of us holding on tight, bodies trembling against each other, as we wonder what will happen next.

NINE

Redfearn carries Penelope back to the VIP suite, lays her down on the bed and draws the blankets to her chin, lingering to tuck a golden lock of hair behind her ear.

Then we pull up a pair of chairs and wait for her to wake.

She sleeps fitfully, still in the grip of withdrawal from the Steward's feeding. She tosses and turns, sweat glistening on her forehead and in the hollows of her collarbones, pearling the puckish curl of her upper lip. Her brows draw together and she whimpers, calling out softly in her sleep. "Baby, come back, don't leave me . . ."

Redfearn clenches his jaw in a dancing of muscles. And when his daughter's noises change, taking on a less than wholesome tinge as she writhes and slides her feet about in the bed, toes curling, he looks away.

"You don't have to be here for this, you know." He flicks a glance at me, embarrassment flushing his neck. "This could get—"

"Nonsense," I say primly, as if to a stewardess who has made an exceedingly silly comment, and lift my nose as I stare straight ahead. "Of course I'll be here."

I can feel him studying my profile, perhaps waiting for me to turn, to engage further in this conversation. I don't.

Smiling to himself, he turns away to follow my gaze. But after a moment, I slip my hand into his, fingers interlocking, and squeeze tight.

After perhaps an hour, Penelope's writhing slows and stops, her breathing deepens. For a moment, I think the feverish nightmares have ended, that maybe she's gotten through the worst of the withdrawal.

Then her eyes crack open.

She jolts upright in bed, red-rimmed eyes flying about the room. "Where am I? Why—" Her eyes narrow as she recognizes the suite. "Why am I back on the *Thing*?"

Redfearn swallows, spine stiffening in his chair. "It's a long—"

"I need to go to him." She sweeps the comforter back and hops out of bed, makes for the door. "He'll be looking for me. I can't make him worry."

Redfearn shoots to his feet and steps in front of her, grabbing her by the arms. I rise also, hands twisting at each other, not knowing what to do.

"Sweetie," Redfearn says. "You're confused."

"The fuck off—" Penelope's face falls as she locks eyes with her father, seeming to drift out of some fugue state. A furrow forms between her brows. "Dad?"

Redfearn drags in a ragged breath and nods, his lips wavering up in a smile. "Hi, honey."

"You . . ." She narrows her eyes, putting it together now as if emerging from a fog of amnesia. "You took me from the castle."

Redfearn nods again, hope filling his features. "Yes."

"You took me from him."

Redfearn stills.

Penelope's eyes darken behind the tangle of her hair, dull with hate.

Then she rears her hand back and slaps him across the face.

The force of the blow is strong enough to rock his head back and to the side. I take an involuntary step forward, my heart leaping into my throat, but Redfearn holds out a staying hand: *No.*

When he looks back at his daughter, his cheek mottled red and already puffing up, she leans in close, the words low and seething: "Fuck you."

Redfearn's eye twitches.

After a moment, Penelope straightens, lips thin, and makes a curt gesture. "Out of the way."

Redfearn's voice, when it comes, is weary with resignation. "I can't do that, honey."

Penelope glares at him, nostrils flaring, chest rising and falling in deep, controlled fury. Then she makes a dash for it, trying to get around him, but he's ready for this. He catches her, and for a moment she struggles in vain, hands flailing, slapping at the unyielding solidity of his body, before she gives up and wrenches away, hands lifted in the air. *"Fuck!"*

I stand there with a hand to my throat, unable to breathe around the stone in it.

Penelope paces in a circle with her hands on her hips, her breathing as noisy and irregular as a trapped animal's in that room. Redfearn watches her with sorrowful eyes.

"You had no right," she seethes.

Redfearn drops his head, bobs it in acceptance if not agreement. "I'm sorry. But I can't let you go back to him."

She spins at him. "Why?"

Redfearn sighs, the sound of a man who knows he has to say a terrible thing. "He's a monster, Pen."

Penelope's teeth clench, a flash of angry white. "Don't you speak of him like that."

"He's a slaver. He brings girls to that castle so he can—"

"Shut up."

Redfearn gives her a long, steady stare. "You know it's true."

But Penelope shakes her head, lip upturned. She crosses her arms tightly over her chest. "You're lying."

"He hired me. With *this* boat." Redfearn jabs a finger at the floor, a hint of anger in him now. "The boat you once worked on. He had me pick up a pack of girls your age or younger to bring to him. Which means every time you worked a passage there, you were—"

"Lies. More lies."

Redfearn crosses his arms now, matching her obstinancy. "You really believe you were alone in that castle?"

Penelope's chin trembles, just the slightest bit, a hint of vulnerability in her glassy eyes. "He only loved *me*."

Redfearn lets out a low, exhausted sound of frustration and glances at me, pleading.

Anxiety dumps into me. The fear that I'll let Redfearn down, that I won't reach his daughter. That I'll only make things worse by getting in the middle.

But she has to know.

I step forward with hands clasped before me and clear my throat. "He doesn't love anyone, Penelope. He is not capable of love."

Penelope looks me up and down, a faint sneer curling her lip. "And how are you the expert again?"

Redfearn shoots me a worried look, but I don't return it. I lift my chin, poised and refusing to allow shame to creep into my voice. "Because he's my ex-husband."

All color drains from Penelope's face. Her eyes widen. "Bullshit."

It's the best reaction I can hope for.

"He made me feel special, like you," I continue, unperturbed. "When he showered me with his attention, it was like the sun on my face. I had never been happier."

Penelope, I realize, is hanging on my every word. As is Redfearn.

I cannot look at either of them.

"But that's what he does. Lures you in, gets you hooked on his love, before he shows you the real Mr. Colding. And by then, it's too late. You're under his spell. You cannot live without him. Because your entire world rests on his approval and validation. You are nothing without him, and he is nothing without you." My voice is threatening to get away from me, and I take a moment, wait for it to pass. "He would have killed me rather than let me go. And he tried to." I look down, gooseflesh puckering my arms. My voice drops to a curt whisper. "And that was before he was changed into the creature he is now." I take another step forward, look at Penelope boldface. "I can't let you go through that. I wouldn't be able to live with myself."

Penelope stares at me in the following silence for what seems like an eternity.

Then she draws in a breath.

"I think," she says, "it's kinda sad you never got over him."

I stiffen.

"That's right. I heard what he called you, *little empress*." Penelope's eyes flash with a hateful light. "You just want him for yourself. And you're too infatuated to see he's just fucking with you in order to get me back."

Redfearn takes a step forward. "*Penelope*."

My heart beats against the back of my throat, a tiny, terrible thought flickering inside me—*Is she right?*—before it's gone.

Penelope is still staring at me, arms crossed, pugnacious even while there's a hint of regret behind her eyes.

"You don't know these things like we do, Pen," Redfearn interjects. "We just wanted you to be safe. *I* wanted you to be safe."

Penelope turns her gaze on him. "And what gave you the right to decide that?"

"Because I'm your father."

Penelope gapes, a sick smile twisting the corners of her mouth. "My father?" She utters a harsh burst of laughter. "That's rich. So you got it into your head that I needed saving, and now that you've done it, you think this will somehow make up for what you did? You fucking *abandoned* me, *Dad*. You abandoned me, like the coward you are, and now you've taken me from the only man who ever loved me. And I'm supposed to be fucking *grateful?*"

Redfearn flinches as if slapped again, tears filling his eyes, and a cool, indignant anger possesses me.

"That's not fair," I intone, assuming—for the first time in this conversation—my stern chief stewardess voice. It roots Penelope to the spot. "What do you expect him to do when he knows you're in danger? Just sit around and ignore it? He did what any father would. But not all of them would go through the hell he's gone through to do it."

Penelope shifts her weight, fighting through a wave of guilt despite herself. Then juts her chin in a defiant angle. "You supposed to be my new mother or something?"

This stings far, far more than I thought it would. But I don't let it show as I meet her gaze head-on.

"I've seen him fight things that would make you piss yourself, dear. I've seen him fight bloodsucking terrors. I've seen him fight alcoholism. I've seen him fight his gambling addiction. I've seen him struggle with the hate he holds for himself. And every day he gets up and tries to be the man he never was for you, because he has never forgiven himself for it. He is the strongest man I have ever had the honor to know, and I will be damned if I stand here and let you talk to him that way."

By the time I'm done, uncertainty and what may even be a hint of respect have crept into Penelope's glare. Her posture has not changed, her hands still on her hips, though her eyes have taken on a glassy quality. She sidles them at her father.

Redfearn has turned puce, his shoulders slumped in a hangdog look. He looks between us, his gray eyes tender and grateful as they fall on me.

Then he faces his daughter.

"I don't know if I can ever express how sorry I am for what I did to you."

She jerks at this, the muscles around her mouth twitching, her eyes getting shinier.

"I want you to know it was me." He places his hands to his chest, one over the other. "Me. Not you. My leaving was in no way a lack of love for you as my daughter. It was—my father—" He looks up at the ceiling so as to keep the tears from falling and takes in a deep, wavering breath.

Tell her, I urge him silently, a painful lump forming in my throat.

When he speaks again, he lifts his hands as if approaching a wild foal. "My father taught me to hate myself. And that is no excuse for leaving you. Only to explain that I didn't feel good enough to be your father. And I thought—I thought you'd be better off without me. And so my charters got longer and longer, and every time I left, it broke my heart. Seeing your face, knowing you would make presents for me and leave them under the Christmas tree, wait to give them to a father who never came home . . ." His face twists and he covers his eyes with a hand, his forehead turning bright red, and Penelope looks away, her lip trembling.

When Redfearn speaks again, I can barely see him. My eyes have blurred up.

"I knew I was hurting you," he says, his voice cracking. "And the longer I stayed away, the more it seemed to be a mercy. To spare you the pain of having your hopes dashed. And so your mother and I decided I should stop coming home altogether."

The trembling of Penelope's lip has gotten out of control, and she shakes her head, no, no, no. A tear slips down her cheek and she dashes it away with vicious force, as if to deny its existence.

"I'm so sorry I wasn't the father you deserved," Redfearn goes on, taking a tentative step closer. "I'm so sorry I left you. You can't know how much I love you, how hard I've tried to be a better man for you, how badly I've wanted to just hold my little sun again—"

"Stop," Penelope whispers, hiccupping the word, and lifts a finger. Redfearn freezes in his tracks. "No. Mm-mm. You don't get to say that. I needed this version of you when I was a kid. When it fucking *mattered*." She gasps in ragged snatches of breath, clinging to a hard, small, indestructible anger that's kept her going for years. "I don't need you now. I don't love you now." And her eyes go cold as her voice steadies, stripped of all emotion. The blank stare of the forsaken. "I lost all love for you a long time ago."

Redfearn takes this on the chin like an old, weary boxer who has seen every move, every feint and jab, and sure as bloody hell anticipated this one. Then he shakes his head, back and forth. "I know that's not true." He opens a closet and reaches up, drags out a cardboard box and sets it on a table. There's a name scrawled in black marker on its top: PENELOPE.

The box she left with her best friend, back in Fort Lauderdale. He must have brought it with us, kept it in this room, all this time, in hopes of having it here for her should he succeed in his mission.

Redfearn unfolds its flaps and lifts out a small rectangle of glossy cardstock, a vintage illustration of Sardinia flashing on one side.

Penelope, recognizing it, stiffens all over.

Redfearn rubs his thumb across the faded words he'd written to his daughter years ago. "You kept my postcards. Every one of them." He looks up at Penelope, eyes red and aching. "You wouldn't have done that if you'd stopped loving me." And he shows her the card: at the bottom the words *my little sun*, and beside it a stick figure drawing she'd made years ago, as a child, of her and her father holding hands, her head raying out yellow streaks of light. "You're my little sun, remember? So I could always find my way back to you." The corners of his mouth lift, trembling, into a loving smile. "And now I have."

Penelope stands there, her face scrunched up, chin quivering, the tears streaming unchecked out of the corners of her eyes. Then she lets it out in a small, ragged whisper: "Daddy."

The postcard is set on the table, and Redfearn slowly approaches his daughter, closer, closer, until she takes the final step into his arms, her fingers fisting in his shirt.

"I missed you," she says, choked and muffled, into his chest.

"I know," he says, kissing the top of her head. "I missed you, too. I love you, sweetheart. I'll never let you go again."

She burrows herself deeper into him, shoulders shaking, and Redfearn holds her, his cheek laid on her head, swaying in place. When he looks up at me, the happiness blazing out of him like a supernova, we both beam at each other. I cannot speak, can barely smile for the sobs that want to burst out of me, fill up this room with my joy. For him. For what has happened. This sweet miracle.

He's been made whole again.

Thank you, he mouths at me over his daughter's head, and I mouth back, *I love you*.

TEN

They spend the next hour talking, commiserating, catching up. They bond over the absurdities of yachting, of meeting outrageous demands, pleasing unpleasable owners, both of them laughing. Penelope talks of her time walking the docks, doing boat washdowns, a few charter trips to the Keys and the Bahamas. After she speaks of getting placed on the *Thing*, though, she falls silent, the tips of her ears turning red.

Redfearn rests a hand on her knee. "You don't have to tell us if you don't want to, honey."

"No, I—I want to." She slides one palm against the other, something I've seen her father do, and takes in a grounding breath.

Then she tells us.

"I didn't meet him the first time. It was after. Maybe my third trip? I didn't think much of all the models we were bringing—you see a lot of sugar babes in this industry. One day a model forgot her bag, though, so I fetched it and ran after her into the castle. That turned out to be what started it all." She can't look at her father. All she can do is stare down at her sliding palms. "He was so kind.

He made me feel seen. I'd never—I'd never felt that way before."

A wave of revulsion crashes over me.

"He asked me if I'd ever modeled. I was very flattered. When I laughed and said no, he suggested I try it out, and I kept refusing. But every time I went, I'd bring the luggage and we would talk. He wasn't like the boys back home. He was interested in me. What I thought, what my dreams were. He was respectful, and did not hide his age. I liked that. I liked that he was older. It made me feel . . ." She glances at her father and shifts her weight, steers her story back on track. "Our talks grew longer and longer, and the captain—what was his name?"

"Seamus," Redfearn growls, grinding his teeth.

"Right." Penelope notes his fury at that Irish skipper and old friend, guilty understanding in her eyes. "I could tell he was getting uncomfortable. And scared. But he was too afraid of Mr. Colding to intervene in front of him. When I was back on the boat, Seamus asked me to stay away from him. Leave yachting altogether. But I was stubborn. For the first time in my life, I had found something that made me happy, and I wasn't about to give that up. So when Mr. Colding finally kissed me, I didn't refuse. And when it didn't stop at kissing . . ."

Penelope's cheeks are on fire now. Her palms are all but scraping against each other, and Redfearn reaches out, stills a hand by engulfing it in his own. She grips tight as she goes on.

"When I woke, I felt . . . tired. Lethargic. My neck hurt, but I didn't care. He was there with me. He was kissing me all over. I was so happy. And when he dipped his head to my neck and I felt a sharp pain, I didn't mind so much. As long as I was making him happy, too."

As Penelope speaks, something is working itself upon me. A strange and terrifying recognition. A spine-chilling prickling of déjà vu.

It sets my heart pounding. It creeps my flesh.

I don't know what to do with it.

Penelope takes a moment to compose herself before going on. Her eyes well, her hand turning white as it grips her father's.

"The days began to blur after that. I didn't even realize for a while that I wasn't going back on the boat. At that point, I didn't care—I was where I belonged. By his side. In his bed. It was strange there, like a dream. Time worked in ways that did not make sense. At whiles I'd hear footsteps in the castle. More models being ushered in. And Mr. Colding wouldn't let me see, telling me I was nothing like them. Sometimes I heard screams and told myself I was imagining things. Everything had to be okay, though. Because he wanted me there. He told me he wanted to be with me. He told me he wanted to marry me. Make me his Mrs. Colding."

They both flick a glance at me, and my face turns scarlet. I feel like an intruder. An interloper. An impostor.

A fool.

Something like embarrassment—or, worse yet, something unseemly—squirms inside me, and I clasp my hands in front of me and look down.

Penelope can't do it anymore. She gives her father a pleading look. "I can't—"

"It's okay," he says, putting his other hand over hers and smiling. "You don't have to."

She nods and swallows, giving her father a small, appreciative twitch of her lips. "What about you?"

He knows what that means: Time to switch tack. To distract her from all—*that*. So he tells her about the *Lair*, about Adrian and how we found Arie to break him loose from his grief. (He does not yet divulge their quest to take down the Commodore, which I think prudent.)

And he tells her about us.

She looks at me, an unreadable expression in her eyes—something like a bittersweet happiness for her dad. And I know she must be thinking of her mom.

I don't know what to do. I don't feel like I belong here. I feel as if I shouldn't be privy to this conversation.

I revert back to my old stewardess tendencies and excuse myself, rummage up some food from the galley and bring it to them, excuse myself again.

I pace the passageway outside, brimming with tentative joy at this turn of events. It's a good thing she opened up and shared her story. A first but enormously important step. This will all work out. It has to.

I tell myself I'm not responsible for what she went through.

I tell myself her story didn't stir up something dark and ugly in me.

The next time I return, Redfearn is tucking his daughter into bed as if she were a child again. She looks beyond exhausted.

"We'll talk tomorrow," he promises and leans to kiss her brow, take her face in his hands. "I'm so proud of you for finding the strength to leave him."

She looks up at him, small and hushed, her eyes dark with pain and something else. She smiles.

"I love you, Penelope."

When Redfearn strides to the door, Penelope's eyes meet mine, and I flutter my fingers in a little wave. She waves back.

We shut the door.

We don't bother showering, even changing our clothes. We collapse on the bed in Redfearn's quarters and curl against each other, touch each other's faces and smile, before our eyes slide shut, heavy as those who have survived an inconceivable undertaking, achieved an unspeakable happiness.

We tell ourselves we'll wake early, siphon fuel from a neighboring boat into the *Thing*. Be ready to leave before dawn.

But the exhaustion of joy is too great to even set an alarm, and we're asleep at once.

ELEVEN

I dream of Penelope.

In my dream, she's still in bed, which seems to float, suspended in a primordial darkness. She's curled under the silken sheets, a small, vulnerable form seen only by a predawn glow beginning to creep in through the shades and touch her face with fingers of palest light, as if she were a being in a coffin. And like some put to rest, her sleep is not restful. She twitches, jerks, turns this way and that, caught in the teeth of a dream. Her brows pinch as she encounters something distressing. "No, no," she whimpers and shakes her head. "I'm loyal . . . I didn't want to go . . ." Her breathing deepens, her breasts glistening with sweat as they rise and fall inside her nightdress. "Where are you? Are you close?" Panting now, dragging in quick, hot breaths like a sick dog. She nods her head on the pillow, solemn as a choir girl. "Yes, I'll be good . . . I'll come to you . . . Just tell me when . . ." Crooning now, the fervent, fevered promises of a lover. "Just tell me, Master . . ." And as dawn's furnace glow strikes her face, flushing it as red as a devil in an opera, she gasps as if sucking in the first rattling breath of life, her arched chest lifting her off the bed, and her eyes fly open to reveal they've gone as white and blind as marbles . . .

I wake with a start, my heart slugging in my breast.

It's full morning, and bright sunlight is blasting through the shades of the small captain's quarters onto the bed. Redfearn is beside me, eyes wide, having just woken himself. We lock eyes, and I instantly know: We both had the same dream.

We leap out of bed, out of the quarters, down the glass stairs encircling the elevator descending through the yacht. Redfearn peels off for the guest suites while I march through the double doors and outside onto the aft main deck, the sun a painful glare in my eyes. It's everywhere. Bouncing off the fiberglass hulls of the listing yachts about us, off the water that's blazing in patches of dreamy, tropical turquoise along the atoll reef, a darker blue as it gets deeper inside the lagoon.

I raise a hand and squint, scanning the horizon as I pray, over and over, in my head: *Let him not be here. Let that dream not be real. She's only in the galley, or walking the deck to get some fresh air. He didn't somehow reach out to her through her dreams. He wasn't communicating with her. He didn't lure her away from us right under our noses—*

And then I see it. Through a break in the crowding boats, only half a mile beyond the rim of the Graveyard of Lairs: the Steward's yacht.

The sight of its red sails makes my chest grow tight, my pulse knock in my ears.

Was it real, then? Was he calling to her?

Does he have that power?

My arms bristle with gooseflesh, and I jump when Redfearn speaks behind me.

"She's not there." He's white-faced and out of breath, his silver hair standing up as if he's just dragged his hands through it. "She's not in her cabin."

Then we hear the splash below us.

We both run to the aft rail and look down.

The door to the tender garage is open, and a Jet Ski is idling in the water. Penelope, still in her nightdress, straddles it with one hand on the ignition switch.

Redfearn goes rigid. "Pen!"

She jerks her head up at us, and her eyes have the glazed and vacant look of a sleepwalker.

"Please." Redfearn shakes his head, his long and harrowed face begging. "Don't do this."

Her mouth twitches—a shadow of herself, trapped somewhere behind those frighteningly blank eyes—but whatever trance she's in the grip of is too strong. She turns the ignition switch, throttles the Jet Ski and roars away in a rooster tail of water.

"Pen! *Pen!*"

Redfearn hurls himself down the teak stairs to the swim deck and inside the tender garage. I follow him, going straight for the next Jet Ski in line on the chocks, my hands tugging at the straps tying it down.

"No."

I whip my head at Redfearn. "Don't you—"

"She has a head start." Redfearn has opened a gullwing door in the hull and is operating a small crane, swinging out a strange-looking tender boat and lowering it into the water. "This is the only way to catch up."

I glance back at the Jet Ski blasting away, lift a hand. "But we're losing—"

"Just trust me. Get in."

The harsh decisiveness in his voice snaps my jaw shut. I run over to him and hop barefoot into the tender, and in a moment he's followed and is unhooking the three leg straps of the lifting harness from the crane clip, letting them drop into the floor of the boat. Then he's in the cockpit behind the windshield and is gunning us out of our berth into the graveyard, so fast I'm sucked back into my seat beside him.

But we don't follow the fading wake of Penelope's Jet Ski. We're cutting straight across the Graveyard of Lairs.

"What—" I gesture, whipping my head around.

"We don't have time to catch up to her," Redfearn growls, blasting us through a narrow channel between two tilting superyachts. "She's already outside the graveyard."

And she is. I can see her now. She's banking out of the reef where the water is a swirl of many colors. There's a rising whine and she revs up again, her dress and hair whipping behind her as she follows that curve of sand to meet up with the Steward's boat.

Redfearn's face is grim as he watches her. "Our only chance is to cut her off."

And that's when I see that we're heading dead between Penelope and the Steward's boat. Only we're still inside the atoll ring.

And we're heading straight for it.

"Redfearn," I say in a low, warning voice.

"It's okay," he says, ramping up the throttle until I feel my guts slam back against my spine. "Just trust me."

The bar of pale gold sand flies toward us. Thirty feet away. Twenty feet. Filling up the world.

I brace my hands on the cockpit dash. *"Redfearn!"*

"Hold on," he growls.

And just when the nose of the tender is about to smash into the reef and explode, Redfearn presses a button.

There's a hydraulic whir, and something gains traction on the seabed with a lurch and *lifts* us dripping out of the shallows, spewing wet sand. We're flying across the reef. We're *driving* over it. Impossibly, seamlessly, we've transitioned from seagoing mode to landgoing mode. I crane my head over the gunwale and look down to see rugged, motorized wheels roaring across the hard sand, popping small rocks to powder beneath them. Those monstrous treads had been hidden in molded depressions in the hull all along, ready to be deployed like some superspy's toy. Because we're sitting in an amphibious tender.

I gape in awe at Redfearn, equally infuriated and impressed—and stiffen when I see what's ahead.

A low stone escarpment, jutting out over the far side of the sand reef like a ramp.

Redfearn steers for it.

Penelope looks like she's on a collision course, the hull of her Jet Ski skipping across the waves. We just might make it. If we get on the far side, we might cut her off.

She sees us and the color drains from her face. Then she hunkers down lower and throttles her engine to a roar, her Jet Ski blurring to a velocity that looks ready to break the sound barrier.

And Redfearn floors it, the engine's rumble vibrating into our organs, those rugged wheels climbing up the escarpment until there's nothing under them, and we're airborne.

My insides drop, becoming shapeless and strange. I brace my hands on the cockpit again, a scream caught in the back of my throat.

While beside me, Redfearn pushes a button, retracting those wheels up into the hull again like an airplane's landing gear, preparing us for what's next.

For a giddy, endless moment, the wind whistles in our ears, the water rushing up at us. Penelope nears, and nears, and nears—

And bombs past just as our hull slaps down into the water in a blast of spray.

Redfearn curses and yanks the wheel starboard, hand-over-handing it to swing us about a dizzying ninety degrees.

And we're met with the Steward's boat looming before us like an exotic battle destroyer.

Something at its bow burps flame and a hail of gunfire sweeps toward us, little jets of water popping up from the sea until the bullets rake along our boat, peppering it with holes and cracking the windshield. I shut my eyes and cover my face, letting out a small cry as tiny glass splinters blast across my cheek. Then I'm flung into the cockpit wall as we turn again, Redfearn swerving us out of that line of fire. "Mother*fucker!*" he hisses, craning his head back to see.

But Penelope's Jet Ski is gone. She's nowhere to be seen.

"Where is she?" Redfearn barks, the words swelling with a sob behind them. *"Pen?!"*

There's the throaty gearbox growl of racecar engines and what looks like a high-performance powerboat skids away from the Steward's yacht, sending up a curling fan of water in its wake. It's a tender boat, though unlike any I've ever seen. Slick and mean-looking, its colorway pure black and bloodred, the light glaring off its marine grade epoxy finish. It has a cockpit with a wraparound windshield tinted black as a limo's and a protective T-top to hide the pilot from the sun. And I know who the pilot is.

The back of it is open, showing the Steward at the helm. And who's beside him.

Penelope.

She glances over her shoulder and sees Redfearn, turns to him. That dazed expression on her face has been wiped away. She's been freed from her trance, and she looks terrified.

"Dad!" she screams.

Redfearn shoots to his feet, veins standing out on his neck as he grips the windshield. "Pen!"

But a pale hand grabs her arm, and the Steward grins over his shoulder at us.

Three 450R Mercury Verado outboard engines rise to a thunderous whine and blast the powerboat off in soaring skips across the waves, heading for the coast of China.

"Peeeennnn!" Tears glisten in Redfearn's eyes, his voice turning into a ragged howl of pain that tears at my heart. "I'll follow! Wherever you go, I'll find you!"

A sob is bubbling up from my chest. This can't be happening. This is a nightmare.

Then I see something flash white on the Steward's boat: the scope of a sniper rifle.

I haul Redfearn back down into his seat just as the bullet zips through the windshield where he'd been standing. It blurs past us, a bee of hot metal, and buries itself in the aft cushioning, sending up a puff of stuffing.

Sunlight flashes off of something else now: the Steward's bullhorn. "Stay where you are," a cold voice blares, "or we will use force."

And as we bob there in the shallows by the atoll, I swallow hard in understanding. "They want to take us alive."

Ice enters my bloodstream.

Redfearn is staring unseeingly through the cracked windshield, his face turning red. His lip snarls up. "Fuck that," he growls in a low, seething rage and grips the wheel.

"Wait." I grab his arm, a sudden idea coming to me. "Do you still have the yacht controller?"

He frowns but rummages in the pocket of his khaki shorts, pulls out the controller. I grab it and hold down its dual power buttons until its lights flash a solid yellow. The *Thing*'s control has transferred to me.

"What are you doing?" Redfearn snaps, curious even through his distracted anger.

"Just keep them occupied."

Redfearn arches a quizzical brow, then looks out at the flashing dot of the Steward's powerboat disappearing into the horizon. A thick band of muscle flares in his temple, and I know he's considering going after him even now, snipers be damned.

But in the end, he slowly stands, hands raised. "Don't shoot," he calls.

I tap the anchor button and wait a moment. And then, taking a deep breath, I slowly ease forward on the thruster controls.

Very faint, I can hear it—the painful screeching of metal and fiberglass.

Redfearn raises his voice to drown it out. "Please. We'll cooperate."

The Steward's yacht is creeping toward us now. With its wind-filled and winglike sails, it looks like a bird of prey swooping down on us.

Somewhere distant, there's a groan of metal, the sound of boats getting pushed out of the way.

"Just don't hurt us," Redfearn calls.

The Steward's boat is almost on top of us. Crew members man its bow, guns trained on us. And someone is operating a crane, preparing to launch a boat to fetch us.

"I don't know what you're doing," Redfearn says out of the corner of his mouth, "but you better do it soon."

I frown in concentration. "Just trust me."

Then I see it. The *Thing*, shouldering its way toward us through the graveyard lagoon. I tap on the controller, redirecting its course.

The Steward's boat slows, almost on top of us. It blots out the sun, its shadow falling over us, raising the goose bumps on our skin as we hear the whine of its crane swinging out a tender boat. The sound of our doom.

"Mrs. Colding?"

And I push both knobs all the way forward and hold them there: full speed ahead.

There's a violent, metal-shearing crash and dozens of heads turn to see the *Thing* ram its way through the outer ring of boats in the graveyard lagoon, knocking vessels aside as it barrels toward the Steward's boat like a runaway train. For a moment, the idea of it is too absurd—too unthinkable—to contemplate. Then the panic sets in, the inexorable reality of it, and there are shouts, curses, crew members dashing across the deck as the boat begins to turn in a desperate bid to save itself.

But it's too late.

The *Thing* explodes into the narrow strip of reef like a bulldozer, blasting sand away from its bow in golden clouds as it rocks upward, its front third catching air as it half sails, half scrapes over the atoll rim like a flying mountain of steel and fiberglass and crashes into the Steward's boat.

I have no reference for the sound the impact makes, a great booming slam that's like the world rending apart. My eardrums throb. My eyeballs vibrate in their sockets. The very air seems to shudder. The *Thing* almost cleaves the Steward's boat in two, shredding her open like a can opener: crumpling her metal, smashing her wooden decks open in a brooming up of splintered beams, tumbling her screaming crew downward into that newly opened hell. Then the sea around those two boats turns white as the explosions concuss the air. Redfearn and I are blown back into our seats, cheeks hot, eyes sweating, the hairs on our arms curling from the heat, and Redfearn shields me with his body as flames boil upward into the sky and engulf that nightmare vessel's red sails, puffing them black and ragged.

When we look again, that pair of hopelessly entangled boats has half-sunk into the shallows in a confusion of wrenched metal and crooked masts dripping rags of scorched canvas. The two most recent additions to the Graveyard of Lairs.

Redfearn and I gape at each other, the wonder and relief filling our faces. We're shaking, chests heaving. The nervy, adrenaline-spiked high of those who have narrowly escaped a terrible fate.

He places a hand to my cheek. "You—you—" He cannot even find the words. Jittery laughter erupts from our mouths.

Then Arnold Redfearn looks out at the blinding horizon, and his face crumbles as he remembers: He's lost his daughter again.

TWELVE

The grief hits him first, followed slowly by rage.

His breathing deepens. His nose wrinkles in a snarl, lips peeling back from clenched teeth, and he raises a hand as if to pound the wheel. But he doesn't. That was the old Captain Redfearn, the one who didn't know how to control his anger. The Captain Redfearn in front of me now stops himself, his hands curling into fists, and rocks forward until his brow is on the wheel. He lets out a great, shuddering breath.

I scoot over on my seat and wrap my arms around him, lay my cheek on his back. "I'm so sorry," I whisper.

"I promised her," he says through a thick clot of tears. "I told her I'd never let her go again."

"And you won't." I hug him harder, biting the inside of my lip to stay composed. "You'll get her back."

It takes him a minute for his deep, ragged breaths to slow and even out. Then he harrumphs and straightens, and I pull back enough to rest my chin on his shoulder, stare at him until he looks at me and gives me a weak smile.

Then he drags his hands down his face, slaps them down onto his thighs and sniffs in hard.

"Okay. Time to get her back." He looks at me, takes my hand in his and traces the folds of my palm with a thumb. He opens his mouth.

"Redfearn." I give him a tender smile. "We've been through this before. There's no way you're telling me I'm not coming with you."

He freezes, mouth open—and lets out a helpless laugh, shaking his head. "Right. No way I'm telling you that it's different now, and that it's too dangerous to drag you into this madness."

I swish my head back and forth. "Nope."

"Because how could I ever be stupid enough to doubt your loyalty?"

"Precisely. How could you?"

We look at each other, small smiles trembling at the corners our mouths. Then he snorts and looks out over the turquoise water. At this place that would be paradise if not for the graveyard of boats, the burning wrecks off our bow. "It's just, your ex has her. How can I make you face him again—"

"On the contrary, that is precisely why I have to do this." My throat narrows, and I have to clear it before I go on. "Not just for you. Not just for her. But for me, too."

Redfearn studies my face before bringing his attention back to my palm, as if he'll find an answer there. "I guess I just—I'm afraid that—"

Heat rises up my neck—the beginnings of embarrassment, or shame. Because I know what he's hinting at, what he can't say aloud.

What he's really afraid of.

I put my other hand over his. "He's a monster, Redfearn. That won't happen."

He eyes me askance, his crow's feet tightening in an expression I can't decipher. Then he snorts, his tone gentle. "We're still calling each other by our last names. We ever going to change?"

"Maybe," I tell him, letting one side of my mouth curl in return. "One day. When we've left the yachting world behind us."

He gives me a dubious squint. "You think you can do that?"

My smile grows wider, turning flirtatious. "With the right person? Maybe. Miracles can happen."

He laughs, a shadow of his old humor crossing his face, and touches the half-moon pendant hanging from my neck. "My sailor moon," he whispers, making my breath catch. Then his voice turns grim. "I'm beginning to be afraid we won't live to see that day. Even if you come with me, we don't even have a yacht anymore." He glances at the useless rusting hulks tilting this way and that in the lagoon, back to our tender pockmarked with bullet holes. "We're outgunned and outnumbered, and they'll know we're coming now. There's almost no hope of coming out of this alive."

We sit there as the amphibious tender rocks under us, listening to the water lapping against her hull. I do know the chances. I know Redfearn has almost zero now without me. And I also know, as if this had been the plan all along, that there's only one way forward now.

My eyes are on the horizon when I say it. "He'll kill you as soon as look at you. But he'll speak to me."

Redfearn turns toward me, and I do the same.

"I might be able to talk him into letting Penelope go."

The captain's face mottles. He opens his mouth to object, but I override him.

"We both know I'm right. I'm the only one he'll speak to. Whether you like it or not, Captain Redfearn, the only way to get your daughter back now is if I talk to my husband."

Redfearn stares at me, lips pursed, on the verge of letting out a sharp retort. Then he glares out the windshield with its spiderwebbing of cracks, his jaw working, muscles pulsing along its strong angles, as the resignation settles inside him like a stone.

I make the phone call on the atoll reef, kicking my bare feet in the hot sand. "Come on," I grit under my breath. "Please have service."

I glance behind me where the amphibious tender is parked, the deep treads of its wheels encrusted with a dusting of gold grit. Redfearn stands a few feet from it, arms crossed, staring out at the ocean. I have never seen a more unhappy man.

The other end finally picks up, and Mr. Chung's voice comes over the line, faint and staticky. "My ice queen. It's a relief to hear from you again. Your venture was a success, I trust?"

A wild urge to laugh takes me. "Not exactly."

"Sorry to hear it." There's a pause. "You're in need of my help again, aren't you?"

You can say that again. "Depending on how things play out, I'll probably be calling you again soon for another favor. But first thing's first: I need you to track down a phone number for me."

It takes ten minutes before I get a text from Chung. When I see the shared contact, my heart starts to pound in my chest. I hover a trembling thumb over it, glance up.

Redfearn is watching me.

I tap the contact and turn around.

He answers almost immediately. "Hello, my little empress."

The hairs on the back of my neck stand on end.

"I knew you'd call." There's a long, gloating silence as my palms dampen with sweat, as if he knows full well, full well, how hearing his voice affects me.

That cheery voice turns mild. "You didn't do anything to my boat, did you?"

I raise a brow at the burning carcass of that Chinese junk, unable to stop a small satisfaction from creeping into my voice. "Not anything you wouldn't have done to me."

"Well. You do lose a few assets in divorce, they say. Weren't content with just taking the house, were you?"

The chumminess, the sickening familiarity of our conversation, suddenly makes me want to puke.

I get us back on track. "We need to talk."

"Oh? I thought we were."

"In person."

"Well, well. All business today, I see. Where and when?"

"One hour. Five miles north of the graveyard. I'll text you the coordinates."

"See you soon, little emp—"

I end the call. Still hearing his soft laughter in my head, all the same.

THIRTEEN

I take the amphibious tender.

Redfearn is too distraught to know what to do with himself. He follows me as I place a foot on one of the tender's tires and haul myself up into the cockpit, seat myself on the driver's side. I punch the power button and the tender comes to life with a juddering hum, all its lights winking on.

"This is a mistake," Redfearn says. "He wants this. You think this was your idea, but it isn't. It was his. Don't do it. Don't go. Stay here, and we'll find another way."

I lean down and hold Redfearn's face in my hands, kiss his mouth. I taste the sea on his lips, or the salt of tears. I rest my brow on his. "I love you," I tell him and sink back into my seat, grab the wheel. "I'll be back soon. I promise."

I ease the stainless-steel throttle handle up and the amphibious tender rolls forward on its wheels, leaving tracks in the sand. I turn her about and face her out to sea, and Redfearn is pacing me as the tender drives into the shallows, one hand pressed to the cockpit window.

I can't look at him. I know if I do, I'll stop to hold him, and I might lose my nerve.

Then the seabed has dropped away from under the wheels and the tender is floating, leaving Redfearn behind. I punch the button for seagoing mode and hear the hydraulic whine of the wheels folding up into their depressions in the hull, clunking into place.

I can't help it—I look back once. Redfearn watches from the reef, arms at his sides, looking as lost and bereft as a marooned sailor. A sudden despair wrenches at me—a feeling that I will never see him again—and I turn away.

My insides have twisted themselves into knots. A grimy sordidness clings to me, a sense of betrayal, and I wonder if this is what it feels like to have an affair. The sneaking and skulking, the pervading guilt, and the thrill because of it. The shameful yet defiant anticipation of a connection outside your union that has the power to bring about a mysterious expansion of the self.

I just want answers, I tell myself. I just want to know that I can face him.

But I have a terrible suspicion there's more to it than that.

When I ease forward on the throttle again, the tender's outboard motor kicks in, taking me out to sea.

It doesn't take long to get there. Far too soon, there's a white flash in the distance, sunlight bouncing off metal, and a shudder passes through me.

I slow the tender to a crawl.

It's the same slick powerboat he left in, her colorful paint job gleaming like blood in the bright daylight. As she drifts slowly around her dropped anchor, her aft faces me to let me see inside her.

He's standing there in the safety of the shadows under that T-top bimini, his eyes glowing like the round reflective panes of spectacles.

My back stiffens. I haven't been this close to him in over twenty years, and still—gooseflesh bristles my arms. My body grows hot and cold in different places. His lambent eyes rove over me, and I feel them like hands on my skin.

I glance away to scan the horizon.

Nothing can be seen out there. Only empty water, patches of it glowing a luminous, tropical turquoise, denoting shallower depths, the seabed only a dozen feet below. Not a telltale flash of metal anywhere.

"Don't worry," he calls from his powerboat. "We're quite alone."

I crank the wheel over so the amphibious tender revolves on the spot until her stern is facing his. Then I kill the engine, pad to the stern and toss the anchor into the water.

As the splash fades, we stare at each other from our tenders across a span of perhaps twenty feet. One of us in shade, one of us in daylight.

That daylight being the only thing guaranteeing my safety.

He knows what I'm thinking. He steps to the edge of the shade, hands clasped behind his back, and squints out at the blazing day like a predator inspecting the perimeter of its cage. Light sparkles off the water, showing me he's changed his clothes, has swapped out that shimmery Oriental robe for a Chinese tuxedo tunic suit with floral designs.

Almost as if he were dressing to impress me.

As if we were on a date.

"After all these years," he breathes, taking me in, "still as beautiful as ever. It almost makes me question which of us is immortal." His eyes narrow as he squints at my neck. "Though I see one of my kind certainly tried to make you one."

The fang mark scars on my neck throb and I clear my throat, determined to not let him get to me. Or for him to see it. I clasp my hands in front of me and give him my blank stewardess stare. "You were already dead when Adrian killed you."

His eyes glow with pleasure. "It's too bad," he muses as if he hadn't heard me, and purses his lips. "I rather think you would have enjoyed it if it had been me."

The scars throb again in a painful, almost pleasurable way, and I shudder, thinking of his lips on my throat, the pricks of his teeth piercing my skin, and feel the draw of a confused but yielding passivity.

I fight this down. "I doubt that."

Far from being affronted, a smirk of almost admiration adorns his full red lips. "You have changed, haven't you."

I lift my chin. "And you're exactly the same."

His glowing eyes crinkle in amusement. "Oh, I wouldn't go that far. I've just grown more . . . *particular* . . . in my tastes." He slides his tongue over a long ivory fang. "And how to enjoy them."

All the moisture dries up in my mouth. I wet my lips. "Is she alive?"

"Penelope?" He frowns, looking disappointed, and glides farther back into the shadows. "Yes, that's why we're here, aren't we? And here I was hoping we would catch up on each other's lives."

"I think I know all I need to."

"Do you?" His eyes flash out of the darkness gathered under the bimini shade. "Don't be so sure. You might like to know that I've spent all these years grieving the end of our marriage. That with every woman I feed on, I hope I can forget you. That every time I wake from my gorgings there is a brief, blissful moment in which I forget that I now live a life without you. And then I remember. I remember I'm in hell."

My eyelid flutters, as if trying to bat away the bewildering turmoil these words have stirred up in me. "I know," I enunciate slowly, "that you'll say anything to get what you want."

Does he know about Adrian's predilections, and why I chose to serve him? I think of Adrian feeding on blondes to remember his wife, and this flip side to dealing with grief.

He's using that against me in this moment, trying to gain my sympathies.

And if what he was saying were true?

Those glowing eyes drift closer again. "Can you honestly say you don't like hearing it? That someone's love for you is so strong, so . . . *obsessive* . . . that it endures for decades?"

My eye is twitching again. I clear my throat.

"Just let Penelope go. I know this isn't about her. This is about me. You want to hurt me for leaving you, for finding love again. I understand. But if you were trying to make me love you, I can assure you, this isn't the way to do it. Just let her go and we can all forget about this."

There follows a long silence. All that can be heard is the wind whistling through the T-top bimini shade, the clink of anchor chains as our boats drift on the swells.

Then: "I don't know about that."

Something round and hard slides down my throat, through my chest, drops into my gut.

"Is she dead? Is that it?" I tremble with the beginnings of a hot, furious rage. "If you killed her, so help me—"

"You answer a question of mine, maybe I'll answer yours. What do you say?"

I press my lips together, fighting to calm my breathing, and he smiles a sharp smile.

Then he asks his question: "Do you still love me, Mrs. Colding?"

I blink, slapped with shock, the outrage of having this be the question I have to answer. I consider lying, but I know that won't be any use. He has always seen through my lies. And this is not the time to anger him.

I take a breath. "There will always be a part of me that loves who I thought you were."

If I thought this would disappoint him, I was wrong. The corners of his mouth twitch in a smug smile as if receiving a compliment, and my stomach goes queasy.

I shove that away. "Your turn."

"Yes," he says, soft with self-satisfaction. "She's alive."

"That's not good enough. I want to hear her voice."

His mouth swells in a sharklike smile, curving fangs gleaming. "As you wish." He takes out his phone and dials, stares at me as it rings. A muffled voice answers. "Hello, sweetie," the Steward sing-songs. "There's someone here who wishes to speak with you." He puts it on speakerphone and holds it out to the edge of the bimini's shade.

There's a hiss and crackle, and then I hear Penelope's voice. "Hello?"

"Penelope?" My heart thuds in my chest. "It's Mrs. Colding."

"Mrs. Colding?" Her voice is slow, spacey, disconnected.

"I'm here, darling. I'm okay. Both your dad and I are okay. And we're coming for you. We're going to bring you back."

"Bring me . . . back?" Penelope draws out the words as if having trouble understanding them. Then a mulish rebelliousness creeps into her voice. "No. I don't want to. I want to stay with Mr. Colding."

The air leaves my lungs. I step to the edge of the swim deck, strain forward. "But, sweetie, your dad loves you—"

"My dad *disowned* me," the voice snarls with sudden spite, then softens into a giggle. "I have a new daddy now."

I put a hand to my stomach. The rocking of the tender is suddenly making me feel sick. "Honey, wait—"

"I think that's quite enough." The Steward taps his phone, ending the call, and tucks it back into his pocket. "It seems pretty clear who she wants to stay with."

My hands claw into fists at my sides as I glare at him. "You fed on her again, didn't you? You put her in some bloody trance—"

"It *was* rather bloody," he admits, inspecting his talon-like nails.

"You goddamn monster," I spit, trembling with rage.

Those eyes flick up at me, dull and flat and reflective as a nocturnal predator's. "You know, I really don't like your attitude right now."

My body goes rigid.

"She's made her choice, and we must respect it. You can't blame her, with a father like that. It's what best for her. She'll be happy with me. I will never hurt her in a way she doesn't ask for. And I will never abandon her like your Captain Redfearn did. You can count on that." He steps forward, his body almost grazing sunshine now. "This is the man you chose over me? How disappointing." His eyes drop to the half-moon pendant on my chest and his lip curls in a sneer. He shakes his head. "But it doesn't have to stay that way."

There's a cool, dry touch at the nape of my neck, as if a hand were gripping there.

"I know you miss what we had. There is a hole in you no man can fill. Why think this Captain Redfearn ever could?"

"He—he's a good man," I find myself stuttering. "He knows who I am, loves me for who I am. We both know I wasn't enough for you. No one is."

He lets out a weary snort of disgust. "Denial, is it?" He sighs. "I know you don't trust anyone anymore. You don't trust in your love, or who you give it to. You're broken. Always have been, always will be. We were made for each other. I have my flaws, as all men do, but at least it's a love you're used to. Wouldn't it be better to settle for what you know than what you don't? With him, there's no knowing what you'll get. There's no depending on it. There's no knowing it will last. But us—we can be trapped forever in this love." He reaches up with both hands and grips the crossbar of the bimini shade, talons clicking against metal, and leans forward to bare his fangs in a terrible smile. "Let me make you mine forever."

I've backed up across the swim deck until my body smacks against the rear seating of the tender. My neck scars burn. My chest heaves. I'm damp with an ill sweat, filled with a riot of all my most horrible imaginings given voice at last. I shake my head, back and forth. "Stop," I gasp. "Stop talking."

"We can call it a trade if that will make you feel more comfortable about it. Penelope for you. Redfearn gets his daughter back, and I get my wife back. Doesn't that sound fair?" His smile floats away into the gloom of the powerboat. "Talk it over with your captain."

FOURTEEN

Redfearn is sitting in the sand on the reef when I return, arms resting on his knees, fists clenched, head down. When he sees me coming, he shoots to his feet.

"What did he say?" he blurts, his voice an octave higher than its usual bass rumble. By my face, he immediately knows something is wrong. "What happened?"

I don't answer. I transform the tender into a car and drive up onto the reef, punch the power button off. Then I climb down and march straight into the comforting solidness of his body, wrapping my arms tight around him.

"What—are you okay?"

"Just hold me," I whisper.

He folds me in his strong arms, holds me there in that embrace that smells of his sweat, the faintest hint of his woodsy aftershave. I try to bury myself in that scent, that warmth, rooting myself again in Arnold Redfearn's love, reminding me of what goodness feels like.

Yes. This is safety.

This is not *him*.

When the shivering of my body subsides and my breathing evens out, Redfearn cups the back of my head in his big, callused hand, drops his lips to my hair.

His tone, when he speaks, is not angry. It has the immutability of stone.

"What did he do to you?"

I take a deep, rattling breath. "Just—what he does." I pull back to look at him, squinting against the sand-flecked wind. "He tried to get inside my head, make me doubt things."

Redfearn looks like he's listening with his whole body, a quivering tension to him. "Like what?" he says, a note of fear in his voice.

(You're broken.)

(We were made for each other.)

(Wouldn't it be better to settle for what you know than what you don't?)

I open my mouth, look at him, shake my head helplessly, a deep, yawning disquiet tugging at my core. "It doesn't matter. It was all lies."

He studies me in the whipping wind, and for a moment I think he's going to press the issue. But he moves on. "And Penelope?"

My heart pinches, and I smooth his shoulders with their gold captain's epaulettes, meet his eyes. "He's not going to let her go, Redfearn."

He nods and looks away. He expected that.

I grip the placket of his white yachtie polo, study the fine weave of cotton there. "But he offered a trade."

I feel his muscles tense under my hands. "A trade?"

"Yes." I can't meet his eyes again. My heart is thudding in my chest. "He'll let Penelope go if I go back to him."

Redfearn takes two slow steps back to eye me fully, his face whitening in shock. He looks as if he's been gut-shot. "You're joking, right?" He sweeps a hand, palm-down, through the air. "Absolutely not. You stopped me from doing the same thing. That's not an option."

I drop my eyes, jerk my head in a nod. "I know."

"You're not—" His eyebrows draw together. "You're not actually *considering it*, are you?"

"What? Of course not," I sniff with a touch of coldness and turn away, arms crossed, my ears burning. "But there has to be another way."

I can feel Redfearn's gaze on the back of my neck, but shut this out. I can't let my mind go there right now.

I have to save Penelope.

"What are you thinking?" Redfearn asks.

"I'm thinking that we have to tempt him with something he won't be able to resist."

"You," Redfearn says flatly.

"Me. Men like him, they never let you go. You will always belong to them, always be their possession. Forever."

"So what do you propose?"

I turn to face Redfearn. "We make him believe he can have me again."

"How?"

I pace along the reef and past Redfearn, head down in thought. "We appeal to his ego, his sense of superiority and control. But it can't be easy. He has to think"—and it comes to me, my eyes widening as I spin to Redfearn—"I'm a prize."

It takes a moment for it to sink in. Redfearn's tanned face turns gray. "No. Don't do that to me. Please."

I lift my arms from my sides, drop them. "Can you think of another way?"

He shakes his head, runs a hand through his salt-and-pepper hair. "I haven't in years—"

I step up to him, grab his shirt and pull him in for a hard kiss. "I believe in you."

We lock eyes, breathless, swept away on a cresting wave of emotion, and he nods at last in agreement.

I take out my phone and call.

It rings once, twice, three times, and I begin to wonder if he's toying with me, if he won't pick up.

Would it be for the best? Maybe this idea is too crazy, too reckless. There'll be no going back from it. No changing it. An irrevocable altering of all our lives. Would I be able to live with myself if it failed?

Would I be able to live with myself if I did nothing?

I'm no longer sure I want him to pick up when he does.

"Missed me already?" That voice, when it comes through, is so smug I could gag.

But not now. Not with this feeling of restless excitement and determination puffing up my chest.

I put the phone on speakerphone and Redfearn steps close to listen. "I spoke with the captain."

"And?"

"We have a proposition for you."

"A proposition." He moves the word around in his mouth as if it were a strange and fascinating morsel, his voice oozing a sly curiosity. "How interesting. Go on."

I meet Redfearn's eyes, place a hand to my stomach and gulp down air. There's no going back now.

I take the plunge.

"Captain Redfearn shares your passion for cards. So how about you gamble for it." I give him a circus master's dramatic pause. "Penelope and I as stakes. Winner takes all."

FIFTEEN

There's a long silence on the line filled with the spit and crackle of distance, and for a moment I think I've made a terrible misjudgment, rolled the dice on Penelope's life and lost.

What will happen now?

Then I can all but hear it: that fanged smile in his voice. "You have a deal."

I let out a breath I didn't know I was holding, glance at Redfearn as I respond. "How can we trust you? How will we know we'll be safe?"

"Simple: We'll play at a neutral ground for vampires."

For a moment, it doesn't click. My mind fumbles stupidly about at various locations in the Lairverse, and then it wallops me in the face, as obvious as a handprint on a yacht window.

My blood runs cold. "*The Palace of the Fang.*"

I glance at Redfearn to find he's turned a ghastly tint of gray.

"Just so." There's a pause. "But it won't be as easy as that. You have until sunset to reach our meeting place before I leave, and you never see Penelope again. Good luck getting there on time."

Redfearn shows me the face of his diver's watch with its two silver hands: 10:23. Roughly eight hours away.

My hand tightens around the phone with fuming strength. I half expect its screen to crack silver and shatter into powder.

There's a soft, malicious chuckle on the other end of the line. "A bit of advice: Remember the casino coin. Remember our . . . *familiarity*."

And the line goes dead.

I stare at my phone with furrowed brow, a deep unease stirring in my gut. "The bloody hell does that mean?"

When I look at Redfearn, though, his profound discomfort makes it clear: He knows. "What is it?"

He works his way up to it, like someone relaying the news of a death in the family. "When I visited *The Palace of the Fang*, I had to show that casino coin to enter, remember?"

"So? We'll just have to find one of those coins and . . ." Redfearn's pained expression makes me trail off. "What?"

"It's . . . not that simple," he sighs, looking almost sheepish. "Vampires don't need a coin to enter. Only mortals do."

"Okay," I say, not following.

"Those coins are only given to—"

The word the Steward used flickers like a neon sign in my mind: *familiarity*.

"—a vampire's familiar," I finish, swallowing. "I need to become his familiar for us to enter the casino."

Redfearn looks out at the sparkling turquoise waters where China must be, his lip snarling. "Why doesn't he just give us a goddamn coin so we can meet him there?"

I'm thinking the same thing. But I know. I knew instantly, I just didn't want to admit it to myself. But now it's descending down from the corners of my mind like a spider on a silk thread, ready to show the venomous red marking on its underside to me. And the back of my neck crawls.

"Because he wants it this way," I breathe at last. "He wants me to go through this. Prove my love for him again, even if it's all a charade. It's a mind game."

"Why the fuck—" Redfearn's face slackens. "He's hoping it'll actually work. That you'll—" He stops, looking at me, and the heated blood rushes into my cheeks.

"So how do I go about doing this?" I say in an obvious attempt to change the subject.

Redfearn looks sick, ready to argue, to call this whole thing off. This is foolishness, after all. This is twisted. The sick game of a disturbed mind. Why would anyone play along? Why would Redfearn *allow me* to play along? What are the chances of the Steward even keeping his word?

But Redfearn is taking something out of the pocket of his khaki shorts and unfolding it. It's creased and damp in places, but I can still see the writing on it, still see the vintage illustration of a cave in Sardinia, bats fluttering out of that dark mouth into an evening sky.

I can still see the stick figures Penelope drew of her father and herself.

Redfearn stares down at the postcard for a long time, the thick paper stock trembling in his hands. Then his shoulders swell, the breath whistling through his nose.

"There's a place," he growls at last. "Where people go to be chosen."

I ask with as much patience and delicacy as I can: "What's it called?"

Redfearn looks up from the postcard, the corners of his eyelids drooping in resignation. "It's called—

PART FOUR:

THE FAMILIAR RESORT

SIXTEEN

They find us at the Graveyard of Lairs within the hour.

They cruise up in a pair of military-grade skiffs, a group of men with weathered, squinting faces, scars that tell of lives long lived on the fringes of society. Some of them in flip-flops, ragged shirts, others in tactical gear and bulletproof vests. They hop into the shallows and pull their skiffs onto the beach, begin to hand off what we asked for, unscrew the fuel cap on the amphibious tender and refuel her from red five-gallon cans of gasoline.

Their leader approaches me. He has a shaved head pitted with old wounds, a tidy black goatee. A mercenary, I know. A black ops veteran. An expert in extralegal skirmishes. He hands me a scrap of paper. "Mr. Chung pays his respects."

I unfold it. It's scrawled with a line of coordinates, latitude and longitude. I fold it back up and tuck it into the pocket of my yachtie skirt.

The leader hooks his fingers into the collar of his body armor, squints at me. "You sure you don't want us to tag along?"

I glance over at Redfearn. He's stopped one of the men with a black case in his arms and has unlatched it, lifted the lid to check the array of weapons fitted into the polyester foam inside. He bobs his head once in approval, shuts and relatches the lid and waves the man on.

"There's no need for you where we're going," I say. "We need to do this ourselves."

The leader purses his lips as he follows my gaze, looking as if he disagrees with this decision. But he nods. "If you need anything else, just call."

"Thank you."

He lifts a finger and twirls it, and the men follow him back toward the skiffs. As they leave purling white wakes behind them, Redfearn looks back at me over his shoulder, and we lock eyes.

It's beginning.

We leave straightaway. Redfearn punches in the coordinates from the scrap of paper into the tender's chart plotter, checks his watch. Seven hours left until sunset.

No time to waste.

We drive the tender into the sea, and Redfearn punches up the throttle to the max.

Chung's men left the weapons cases in the in-deck stowage near the stern—along with food. We're both starving, not having eaten since yesterday. I grab the grease-stained paper bags and stagger back down into my seat beside Redfearn, pull out skewers of spicy beef and lamb meat. I know Redfearn isn't a huge fan of beef, so I hand him the stick of lamb and we chew in silence, the wind whipping at our hair and clothes.

When I go to the stern again to find water, I end up finding something else.

"Look at this." I grin, lifting one of them. "Your favorite."

Redfearn glances back at me, snorts when he sees the efoil board with its mast hanging below it, the motor attached there. "Yeah, right."

"You'll get over your surfer prejudice one day," I tell him as I reseat myself and hand him a bottle of water, the cap twisted off for him.

"I don't know about that." He gulps back half the bottle and places it in a cupholder, glances at me. We're both thinking the same thing, I know. We're both thinking back on our date. That night we rode those motorized surf boards through a shimmering magic of bioluminescent water, a pod of dolphins accompanying us. It seems so long ago now. A simpler time. A more innocent time. Back before we got caught up in all this wretchedness. A wistful ache moves through me, tightening my stomach, and Redfearn reaches out to hold my hand. He squeezes, and my heart throbs.

Very gently, Redfearn lets go and checks the chart plotter. His broad brow furrows. "It's not that far away. Should only be a couple of minutes now."

I find my heartrate is beginning to climb. I scan the horizon, but can't see anything yet.

Redfearn doesn't seem to see anything at all.

"I was wondering . . ." He gives me a sidelong glance. "You didn't tell me what Penelope said. When the Steward called her."

My stomach goes numb.

"Mrs. Colding?" The rising note of worry in his voice twists at me. "What did she say?"

I look at him, and he inhales long and slow through his nose. "I see."

"I think—I think he bit her again," I explain quickly. "To get her back under his control."

"Uh-huh."

"She still loves you, Redfearn. You saw her on that boat. For a moment, she was lucid. You got through to her. You just can't fight against that—that kind of vampire craft."

His face has screwed up, his eyes shiny. He nods. "Right. So you don't think—they're not sleeping together again—"

"Hey." I reach out to grab his wrist. "You can't think like that."

He lets out a strangled laugh. "What else am I supposed to think about, hmm? She's my daughter. She's my baby girl." His voice cracks on the last two words and he looks away.

"Redfearn." My voice grows stern. "She loves you, okay? She's confused. She's bewitched, but she loves you. You have to hold onto that belief or you're not going to make it through this. Do you understand me?" He looks over at me, restless and wretched and on the verge of despair, and I hold his gaze. My eyes unwavering.

My voice steady. "Hold on, and you'll get her back. I promise."

It gets through. He nods, as if grasping onto a lifeline, and lets out a long, wavering breath, some old training kicking in. He nods again.

"Good." I squeeze his wrist and lean back in my seat, eyes on a flash on the horizon. "Because we're here."

Redfearn turns to look, too, and his face lengthens.

As it turns out, it's not one flash, but two, as the Familiar Resort is shaped like a pair of curved fangs rising into the sky, those high-rises ribbed with balconies and clad in miles of gleaming glass. It almost dwarfs what it soars up from: a small, flat, fan-shaped island that looks like a vampire's smile.

The sight makes me shiver.

Redfearn slows the tender as we approach. The crescent-shaped yacht harbor has jetties jutting out from it to berth a small fleet of superyachts, cruisers, other luxury tenders. And the resort grounds are just as extravagant as its buildings: Those two glittering towers are linked by a series of dramatic, cascading lagoon pools fringed with palm trees. Here and there, thatch-roofed cabana bars pump out sexy rap and pop music, staffed by muscly bartenders in tight white polos. They're not the only ones dressed in white. Waiters drift here and there amid rows of striped sun umbrellas fluttering along the beach, offering trays of fruity cocktails to guests. And the guests, uniformly, are hundreds of stunningly beautiful women luxuriating on sunbeds, baring their glistening flesh for all to see.

And there are plenty who see. When I rummage out a pair of binoculars and case the resort, my back stiffens.

There are shapes lining all those balconies. The shapes of men, also with binoculars, on every floor of both of those high-rises. All watching the sunbathing women with the coiled concentration of predators lurking in high savannah grass.

Despite the heat, I get a chill.

Redfearn's hands tighten on the wheel of the tender. "Now," he growls at me.

I duck into the stern of the tender, come back with one of the weapons cases. I open it between our seats, brace one foot on the dash so my thigh is bared and attach a thin black holster around it, shove a small-frame revolver into it. I do the same with my other leg, this time shoving a push dagger into the holster. I can't help but notice Redfearn looking distractedly over at my legs, and a subtle heat builds in me.

When I cross my legs on my seat again, my yachtie skirt is just long enough to hide the fact that I'm armed to the teeth.

But Redfearn has been busy, too. He selects a long-slide Heckler & Koch P30 pistol from the case, performs a one-handed press check to make sure a round is chambered and tucks the gun into the waistband of his khaki shorts, drops his polo over it.

He looks over at me. "Ready?"

I nod. We're not going to be caught without weapons again.

A dockhand is waiting for us as we drift up to a floating dock link. Like the waiters, he wears a white uniform with a cap, like an old-timey sailor or bellhop, and has the smooth, burnished skin of the rich or those who serve them. He catches our lines and tugs us close until our fenders are bumping against the dock, holds the boat there while Redfearn hops off and helps me after him. As we pass, he doffs his cap, and there's the flash of youthful teeth. "I hope your voyage was agreeable." He ties us off with the deftness of a pro, sweeps a hand. "Please. Follow me."

He leads us down the jetty and across the beach, around the sparkling lagoon pools toward the righthand tower of the resort. It really does give Florida Gold Coast, a sort of Shanghai-meets-Palm Beach vibe. But for all the lavishness on display, it's hardest not to stare at its female clientele. They are the most gorgeous things I have ever seen, hailing from all around the world, plumped and buffed and ready for show. And most of them, it can't be ignored, are no older than their early twenties.

Most of them are Penelope's age.

When I look over at Redfearn, his jaws are grinding, the muscles in his forearms flexing as his fists bunch. I know exactly what he's thinking.

"Penelope would never do this," I assure him in a soft undertone.

"I know," he murmurs, glancing at the dockhand ahead of us.

"She was manipulated. She's not like these girls. She didn't seek this out."

Redfearn doesn't seem to be hearing me. He's staring at the curving tower of the resort looming over us. At all those balconies. All those things with binoculars to their faces, fangs gleaming whitely under them in bated breath, choosing their next victim.

"It's all so much bigger than I thought," he says. "The extent of Volok's reign. It's everywhere."

It is. His apparatus of abuse, and what it does to women. Infiltrating every corner of the globe.

Redfearn is staring at the shining doors of the resort the dockhand is leading us toward. His throat dips in a swallow.

"You don't have to do this," he blurts suddenly. "Go through all this."

My heart softens in understanding. He doesn't know what's beyond those doors. What I'll have to go through. What will be required of me.

Neither do I.

But I can't show any weakness here.

"Of course I do," I tell him and keep my head high, my shoulders back, as I walk on. "This is how I put him behind me."

We've reached the doors. They're massive, made entirely of glass, and the old obsessive-compulsive stewardess in me can't help but admire their fingerprint-free perfection.

Everything about this place is flawless, crafted to be alluring. Just like yachting.

Just like a vampire.

The dockhand turns to us with an apologetic smile. "The gentleman must wait here, I'm afraid."

Redfearn pales. I turn to him, not knowing what to say—

He grips my arm and leans to whisper in my ear. "If anything goes wrong, you shoot first and meet me back at the boat."

I nod my understanding, and then he's leaning away and the dockhand is opening one of those glass portals, is beckoning me inside that gleaming skyscraper with the warm and empathetic smile of a traitor. "Welcome to the Familiar Resort."

SEVENTEEN

The lobby of the Familiar Resort is stunning.

It's like no resort I've ever seen in my yachting travels. A soaring pyramid of white marble walls, a black marble floor, a brutal monochrome that gives it the feel of a spy headquarters. Or the inside of a tooth. Champagne bottles glitter half-buried in the salted ice of a black marble trough, and women wait with crossed legs on slithering white couches, their colorful sundresses or bikinis clashing with the starkness of the space. They clasp their hands on their knees and push out their chests, touch up their makeup or fuss with their hair as they scrutinize themselves in compact mirrors.

It's a waiting room. All these women are waiting to be chosen.

I feel their eyes burning into my back as I approach the receptionist's desk, the marble freezing under my bare feet.

"May I help you?" The receptionist, a small, black-haired woman in a white sheath dress, gives me a polite smile.

It's hard to concentrate on her words. A sea of crystal chandeliers blown into the shape of fangs float above the receptionist's desk. They sway and tinkle lightly in the breeze from outside, flashing as they turn, and the scars on my neck pulse.

"Do you have an appointment with one of our members?" the receptionist goes on hopefully, and gestures toward the girls on the white couches. "Or do you wish to socialize?" Her eyes stray down me, taking in my yachtie shirt and skirt. "You are . . . a tad older than our usual clientele, but I am sure I can arrange a suitable match for you."

There are footsteps, and a man in a sharp cream suit strides out of a corridor and surveys the girls on the couches. They all straighten their spines and smile, fluttering their lashes. The man smirks, offers a hand to a blonde in a luscious monokini. She flushes and takes it, contemptuous with triumph, and follows him back down the corridor as the other girls burn with jealousy.

"Ma'am?"

I snap myself out of it. "No, thank you," I stammer. "I—I came here at the request of Mr. Colding."

The receptionist lifts a finely plucked brow but says nothing. She consults a screen behind her black marble desk, dials a number on a landline phone. Her eyes flick to me as it rings.

Then: "Mr. Colding? I have a prospective familiar here for you?" She nods and hands me the gleaming black phone. "He wishes to speak with you."

I suddenly feel woozy. The tinkling of the chandeliers is much too loud.

I put the receiver to my ear. "Hello?"

"You took longer than I thought you would," his grinning voice says.

Goose bumps pop up on my skin. I see the fine hairs on my arm lift, as if responding to an electric charge in the air.

I swallow. "I always follow through in the end."

"That you do. I hope you find the contract agreeable."

My hand tightens around the phone. "Is that why you really wanted to speak with me? To say you hope I like the terms of my enslavement?"

"Actually, to give you a warning."

Cold fills my stomach. "Are you threatening me?"

There's a burst of light laughter. "Of course not, dear. I merely wanted to give you a heads up. You see, the two of you have been attracting some attention. After your little demolition stunt with my home—which *was* a tad rude—I was approached by some of my yachting club fellows. He was the father of one called Hong-Li. A friend of my late blood son, Pongshu. He says Hong-Li was never seen or heard from again after he went to visit Pongshu on the *Thing*."

That cold spreads ice throughout my insides, raising goosepimples on my skin as I remember the stout face of a gambler with a manbun. One of those Asian vampire bros who boarded the *Thing* unannounced and threatened to drain the models and crew. I remember leading them into an elevator and locking them inside it. I remember sending that elevator into a glass pavilion abovedeck into the full glare of sunrise.

I remember their screams as they were burned alive by the sun.

"You wouldn't know anything about that, would you?" the Steward's voice purrs.

My lips have gone dry. I lick them. "What are you saying?"

I can feel his shrug through the phone. "He asked who did it, where you were. Per the bylaws of our club, I was bound to aid in avenging one of our own. I couldn't not tell him. I'm afraid this aggrieved father has sent out search parties. They've been combing the area to find you."

My skin shrinks. I fly a look out the glass doors of the lobby, suddenly wary of every boat at the jetties, every room in the soaring towers of the resort.

"Don't worry," the Steward goes on, as if he knows exactly what I'm thinking. "I convinced them to spare you. You're going to be my familiar, after all. You're my wife. I love you. I wouldn't ever let any harm come to you."

I snort. "Unless it's your hands around my throat."

There's a dry silence.

I fill it.

"They didn't come to you," I spit, shaking my head. "You went to *them*. You're just using them to get revenge on Redfearn without getting your hands dirty."

He lets out a long, unhappy sigh. "I don't know why you would think that of me. I don't want harm to come to either of you. I'm just telling you out of concern. If I really wanted Redfearn harmed, why would I warn you?"

I bite my tongue, my chest shuddering with uneven breaths. He waits until he knows he won't get an answer from me.

"I hope the two of you make your appointment safely tonight. I truly do. Tick-tock, little empress." There's a pause. "Oh, and one more thing: Remember where fire meets the sea."

And the line goes dead.

I stare at the phone, my hand trembling. I have the fleeting impulse to smash the receiver on the marble receptionist's desk, turn all his riddles and control tactics and possible, bewildering gestures of concern into a dangling piece of destroyed plastic.

Instead, I hand the phone back to the receptionist.

"Please," the receptionist simpers. "Take a seat."

There's no room on most of the couches, and none of the women are making any for me. So I cross to the opposite side and seat myself on an empty couch, barely aware of the glares from the women. I don't care. I'm not thinking about them. I am lost, in a daze.

Outside, seagulls cry. I wonder what Redfearn is doing.

I wonder if he's safe.

I stiffen, fumble out my phone and call him. I have to warn him. I have to let him know of the danger he's in—

But it goes straight to voicemail.

He must not have his phone on him. It must still be on the *Thing*, half-melted by the explosion and utterly useless.

I slide my phone back into my skirt pocket, praying no one finds him.

There's the clicking of heels and the most beautiful woman I've ever seen strides out of the corridor. Like me, she's Chinese, her winglined eyes mysterious almond depths. And unlike me, she wears a stunning qipao blazing with damasked designs.

I suck in a breath.

She wears the dress very, very well. It clings to her, showing off her shapely form, her swaying hips as she saunters past the desk. The receptionist looks up at her and smiles. "Thank you for staying with us, Miss Wang."

But she does not leave. With all the eyes in the room on her, she heads straight for my couch and sits in an elegant crossing of her legs, retrieves a cigarette holder from her purse. She lights up and holds it in, then exhales a stream of smoke toward the ceiling. "I always need a cigarette after a good fuck," she sighs, turning to me. "Don't you?"

We lock eyes, and our mouths twitch up into smiles.

This close, I can see she's around my age, though she could probably pass for a woman in her thirties. It takes a moment for me to realize how much of a rarity it is to see a mature woman in this industry. It's a breath of fresh air, and I can't help but feel a sense of relief. Of kinship.

And then there's her qipao.

"You like it?" she asks, catching my look.

I lift my eyes from those entrancing designs, unable to keep the mix of longing and wariness out of my voice. "It's very beautiful."

She considers me as she pulls on her cigarette, lets out another stream of smoke, and I can't help but think she knows exactly what I'm feeling. "You must meet my designer, then," she says at last, and reaches again into her purse. "Here." She hands me a card. "Tell her Miss Wang sent you. She'll set you up."

"Thank you." I hold the card, remembering how those qipaos made me feel when I wore them, the delicious contouring to my body. And how Mr. Colding ruined that.

When I look up, Miss Wang is watching me.

"It's time to let go of that uniform, anyway," she says, indicating my stewardess outfit with her cigarette. "That isn't who you are, and we both know it."

I don't know what to say. I can't gather any words in this moment.

The corner of Miss Wang's mouth curves up in a small smile. "Waiting to sign your first contract?" she says lightly, tapping her cigarette in an ash tray.

I nod.

"Nervous?"

I look at her, and it's her turn to nod now. Her eyes narrow behind a veil of smoke. "He made you feel weak, didn't he?"

I stiffen.

"You thought he preyed on you because you were easy?" She makes a soft sound of derision and shakes her head. "You weren't weak, dear. Naïve? Perhaps. But not weak. See, that's where our thinking is wrong. They chose us because we're strong. Because they know we can take it. And because it is so much more satisfying for them to break someone who they know are stronger and better than them. That is their triumph." The end of her cigarette glows and traces orange light in the air as she holds it up beside her, eyes narrowed as she studies me. "So the question becomes: How do you take back your power? By being yourself. By embracing everything you were ashamed of, everything they made you want to hide. The person who you forgot you once were. When they know they can no longer control you, you either scare them off . . ." She glances back at the corridor and smirks. "Or you crook them around your little finger." She leans toward me, her confidence flattering, enthralling. "They are boys, in the end. Terrified of a little pussy. Of the power of a woman who cannot be forced to doubt herself. Become that"—she pokes her glowing cigarette toward me as she leans back—"and you will be something to be reckoned with."

I let out a harsh breath I'd been holding for a while, released from a spell. I feel dizzy, as if I've just downed a shot of straight bourbon.

The door to the lobby opens. A uniformed man stands there. "It's time, Miss Wang."

The woman stubs out her cigarette. "Sign the contract," she says, and turns to grab my hand. "Live for yourself."

I fly my other hand over hers, stopping her. "Thank you."

She stills, her mouth twitching up into a thing of glamour and mystery. Then she's gone, striding out the door held open by the bellhop, out into the bright sunshine and the life she has made for herself.

"Mrs. Colding?"

I jerk. The receptionist is standing over me, smiling. "Follow me, please."

EIGHTEEN

The receptionist leads me down a long corridor of reflective black marble, the clicking of her heels echoing off the walls. She does not look back, does not make conversation. At the end of the corridor the double doors of an elevator wait for us. We step inside and she presses the button for the thirty-third floor. The penthouse suite. A long, low humming. At one point the elevator stops for a cleaning lady to get on. She pushes a housekeeping cart. It's stocked with cleaning supplies I know all too well. And in the bottom, a mop bucket, something sloshing in it. Something dark and red. The same red blotches the cleaning lady's white apron.

She gives me a quick, furtive look of fellowship and terror before stepping off again.

That was me, I think, with an uncomfortable twinge of realization. *How did I let myself become that?*

The elevator dings open on the top floor.

Another long hallway. My legs are shaky now, and sweat has begun to collect under my arms. We pass a row of doors, and I slow at one that's been left ajar. Within, a glimpse of a posh suite with curtains drawn against the light. A man stands in a pleated white tuxedo shirt before a mirror, tugging at his tie. Behind him, on the floor, the bare legs of a woman poke around the bed.

My stomach tightens.

At an intersection, the receptionist finally turns to me. "Wait here." She knocks on a door and slips inside.

I try to still the anxious rush of thoughts in my head. What is waiting for me on the other side of that door? What surprise does the Steward have in store for me? And what did he mean by his latest riddle? *(Where fire meets the sea.)* I know I've heard that somewhere, long ago, but can't remember when.

And then there's what was inside that suite—

"Look at you."

I jump, thinking of Hong-Li's father, of the killers he's sent after us, and whip my head around.

A man in a black suit grins down at me, much too close. I glimpse dimples, a pair of long canines, dark eyes that look me over in a flash of entitlement. "Such class," he marvels in a low, rough voice.

Oh.

He reaches for my arm—

And I pull it away, leveling a cool gaze on him that would destroy any of my stews. "Don't touch me."

His eyes hood over, glinting with pleasure—as if enjoying a challenge.

"Don't be like that." His hand blurs, clamping around my wrist and holding me in place. "It is an honor to be chosen." I glare at him, nostrils flaring, as he trails the backs of two fingers down my cheek. "An old bitch like you should be grateful."

My hand drifts to my thigh, begins to lift the slit in my yachtie skirt until I feel the cold touch of steel under my fingertips: the push dagger.

I wrap my knuckles around the small T-grip handle, and—

"This one has been chosen, I'm afraid."

Our heads whirl. The receptionist is standing in an open doorway, her face an inscrutable mask of politeness. "By the Steward," she adds.

The vampire blanches at the mention of that name, releases my wrist.

And unbeknownst to both of them, I drop my hand from the push dagger.

Satisfied, the receptionist gestures, her voice cool and innocent. "Perhaps I can interest you in one of the girls in the lobby."

The vampire glares at me, then stalks off down the hall. The receptionist pauses as she passes, offers an encouraging twitch of her lips. "She's waiting for you."

I catch her eye. "Thank you."

She hesitates, drops her chin sharply in acknowledgment, and then she's gone.

I linger for a moment as I listen to their footsteps fade, trying to calm my nerves and prepare myself. I smooth my skirt, making sure the holsters are concealed, and lift my chin.

I step inside.

It's an office room with backlit onyx panels, a small table at which a woman sits. Like the receptionist, she's also dressed in a white sheath dress, her hair a gleaming black bob cut at a severe angle. Like me, she's Chinese.

She rises as I enter. "Hello. I'll be your notary today." She leans to shake hands, gestures. "Please. Take a seat."

I cross my legs, making sure the tip of that dagger isn't exposed. I fold my hands in my lap, just in case.

The notary links her hands on the table and considers me with her dark brown eyes. "I see that you're nervous. There's no need to be."

I swallow.

She slides a few sheets of paper to the center of the table, turns them about so they face me. "This is your contract. It's fairly straightforward, but I'll go over the bullet points with you." She picks up a pen and meets my eyes. "Ready?"

I stare at the paper, wondering how many women have sat in this chair before me, how many have signed a contract just like this one. Is this how these things get their brides? Is this how Evangeline Voper bound herself to the Commodore?

How many familiars has the Steward had before me?

It comes to me, in a flash of disgust, that this line of thinking is dangerously close to jealousy.

I look up at the notary. "Ready."

She taps the first bullet point with her pen. "You will keep Mr. Colding's confidence with utmost discretion and never disclose his identity or the identity of his yachts."

I nod. That was to be expected.

The pen taps lower. "You will dress as he pleases."

My insides constrict as I think of those qipaos . . .

And lower. "You will allow him to feed on you at his convenience, day or night."

Horror twists my guts. The scars on my neck crawl.

"You will perform sexually at least three times per week, and there is a list of the various services if you wish me to . . ."

I shake my head, mouth clamped against a rising nausea. "I know what they'll be. You can skip ahead."

"You can act as chief stew of his yachts, or not work at all for the rest of your life. The choice is yours."

I sit there, not knowing what to feel about that one. Trying to find the trap in it, but not finding it.

The pen taps again. "When Mr. Colding has no need of you, you are free to go where you please and spend as you please."

What Mr. Colding is this? When did he ever give me freedom?

"You will have a monthly allowance of three million dollars."

I think of living like Miss Wang. Of carving out a carefree life for myself. This is the lifestyle, the freedom, every woman dreams of. This is the dream. This would be the man of her dreams.

If he weren't a monster.

"Mr. Colding understands you have your own needs, and will allow you to take Captain Arnold Redfearn as your lover, if you choose."

I blink. The room has suddenly grown hot, sending sparks and chills up my spine. This, of all things, I did not see coming. Has he really changed? Has he become less possessive over the years?

Would—my mind dared think it—such a life be possible, even preferable? The threat of Mr. Colding appeased, Penelope released and safe again, and me being able to love Redfearn as I pleased. Even able—if I wanted—to see if I my heart had the space in it to also love—

I shove this thought away, flushed with a hot wave of appalling shame. How could I ever think that? How could I be so gullible as to fall for the manipulation in this farce? How could I ever want to—

"The terms of this contract are indefinite and any disputes will be dealt with in arbitration." The notary finishes in a brisk, clipped tone of almost relief. "If you would . . ."

She's not offering the pen. She slides forward something that looks like a call bell, mounted with a small spur of metal.

I know what it's for.

I press the pad of my thumb onto it. There's a sharp prick of pain and I wait for the fat well of blood to collect, press it onto the bottom of the contract beside my printed name and roll it, leaving a bloody fingerprint behind.

The contract is snatched away, and I sit there in an ill slick of sweat, feeling as if I have compromised myself, as if I have somehow cheated on Redfearn.

This is evil. This is how you sign a deal with the devil.

This is how an abuser makes you hate yourself, turns you away from everything until there is nowhere to go but back into his arms.

The notary places the contract before me again, now with a business card attached to it with a paperclip. "To consummate your loyalty to your new master, you must present this contract to the Bloodsmith." She pushes the contract toward me, taps the business card with a black-lacquered nail. "The coordinates."

When I look up at her, she's smiling at me as if I have won a great victory. "I hope you enjoyed your stay at the Familiar Resort."

NINETEEN

Redfearn waits for me by the lagoon pools.

He hasn't been able to keep still. He paces back and forth, hands on hips, shoulders muscled up in nervy agitation. He runs a hand down his face, rasps it across the stubble on his chin. A waiter approaches with a tray of drinks and Redfearn waves him off without looking at him.

I fidget with the crease in the folded-up contract in my hands. I know what's coming. How he's going to react.

I can't blame him. My head is still spinning with the charming truths or mistruths of temptation.

(*My little empress.*)

I clutch Redfearn's half-moon pendant hanging from my neck as if it were a crucifix, hold fast to my slipping sense of self.

(*My sailor moon.*)

Time to stop putting this off.

When Redfearn sees me coming, his eyes widen and he goes to me, grips my arms. "You okay?" he asks, feeling me tremble, and rubs my arms. "What—what happened?"

"I—" I don't know what to say, don't know how to voice this feeling of violation and guilt, of both victory and defeat. I look into his eyes. "I—got what I needed."

"Is it done, then?" He glances down at the contract in my hands. "Are you his familiar? Did you get the casino chip?"

I open my mouth, hesitate, look down at the contract.

His face changes. "What is that?"

"Nothing," I say, twitching it away.

His jaw hardens. "Is that—a contract? To be his—"

"Trust me." I catch his gaze. "You don't want to see it."

His blink is almost a flinch. His hands drop to his sides. He juts his chin. "Let me see."

"Redfearn," I plead in a whisper, and shake my head, my heart twisting. "Trust me."

We stare at each other. His eyes search mine, seeing the pain there, everything I can't bear to say to him, and his lips press together.

He snatches the contract from my hands.

"Redfearn!"

But he turns away, holding me off with a hand, his eyes widening as they quickly scan the document.

His jaw drops. "That sick fuck." He holds up the contract, all but brandishing it at me. "Is this what it was like to be married to him?"

"It doesn't matter," I tell him, my voice catching as I hold his face. "It doesn't mean anything. It's just to get us to the casino."

He holds a hand over his eyes, his face turning red. Then he breaks free, letting out a harsh laugh. "I'm going to kill him." He throws up his hands as if submitting to the inevitable. "That's it. I have to kill him. He defiled and kidnapped my daughter, and now this—"

"Redfearn—"

"Yeah, Adrian was right," he says, ducking his head in a series of caustic nods. "Oh, yeah."

The name roots me to the spot. "Adrian?"

He puts a hand on his hip, stares at his deck shoes. "I had a phone call with him recently. When I needed guidance on what—what I was going to do about Penelope." He glances at the contract again, looks away as if he can't bear to read what's there. "He said that if Arie is going to take down the Commodore, we need to dismantle his legacy. We destroyed his castle, and that was a huge blow. But the Steward—he's a loose end that needs to be taken care of." He turns to me, eyes shining with unshed tears and a fatalistic joy and resolve. "And yeah, I'm thinking I'm all right with that."

I do not know how to even begin to answer this. A stillness has settled over my once-nervous limbs, communicating alarm, or pride. (*Dismay*.) But I cannot chance unpacking this right now. I fear being waylaid with uncomfortable truths.

I gather Redfearn into my arms, pull his head down into the crook of my shoulder, my fingers tangling in his sterling-silver hair, kneading his scalp. "I love you," I say into his ear.

He drags in a deep, fragile breath, then wraps his arms around me, crushing me to him.

"I hate him," he confesses in a muffled, ragged whisper. "I hate him for what he did to you. What he's still doing to you."

I stroke his hair, my heart hushed and trembling against my ribs. "I know. We'll defeat him," I promise. "Together. We'll find a way. We'll make sure he never does this to anyone again."

He nods into my shoulder, his arms tightening around me. Then he lifts his head, sniffs and smiles at me.

I almost don't have the heart to break it to him.

"There's one more thing, Redfearn."

The captain stills, bracing himself.

"You know those friends of Pongshu's that I—that I took care of? One of them was the son of *The Palace of the Fang*'s owner. And he wants revenge. He's combing the South China Sea looking for us."

Redfearn's face loses color. He already knows, but he asks anyway. "Who told you?"

I blink at him, trying to convince myself not to feel guilty in this moment. "The Steward. He convinced them to spare me. But you—"

Redfearn looks away, muscling down a great agitation in his face. He doesn't need me to say anything more.

"They'll be coming for you." I glance about at all the watching eyes on the balconies of the resort, unable to keep the urgency out of my voice. "We have to get out of here. Now."

He nods, his shoulders rising in a big gathering of breath. "So, what's next?"

I gently remove the contract from his hand. "One more step and I'll be his familiar, and can enter the casino. We just need to pay a visit to whoever this guy is."

I pull the business card free from the paperclip on the contract and we both look at the title printed there in neat Gothic typeface: THE BLOODSMITH. I turn the card over.

On the back, a line of coordinates. And above that, it reads—

PART FIVE:

THE FORGE
OF THE
BLOODSMITH

TWENTY

When we disembark from the Familiar Resort, it's two o'clock.

Six hours until sunset.

Punching the coordinates for the Forge of the Bloodsmith into our chart plotter, we realize it's off the island of Hainan. That's two hours in the opposite direction from *The Palace of the Fang*.

"How long does that give us?" I ask.

Redfearn squints, doing the calculations. "We'll have maybe an hour to spare by the time we get to the palace, if we go at top speed and don't encounter any hiccups."

I frown at the tender's glowing console. "That's not a lot of leeway."

"Best get to it, then," Redfearn growls, and ramps up the throttle.

It's hard not to notice the heads turning as we slip away from the jetty, feel all the eyes on us and wonder if any of them know who we are. If any of them are our pursuers.

I watch for a long time as the island and its gleaming resort grow smaller and smaller, fading into the distance. But I don't see anyone following us.

I find some sunscreen in the dash and we lather ourselves up, knowing we'll be baking in the open for the next couple of hours. Then I settle down into my seat beside Redfearn, watching the dipping horizon as we skip across the waves. We're going full out, almost fifty-five knots, the engines rumbling high and mean and muscular as we blast across the South China Sea, leaving a wake of angry white froth behind us.

We both keep scanning the horizon for any hint of other boats. Anyone moving to intercept us.

Despite this thrum of dread and the frightening bumpiness of the ride, though, I find my eyelids drooping. The fear, adrenaline and bursts of euphoria today have made me beyond exhausted. Before long, my yacht stewardess ability to sleep through anything kicks in, and I'm nodding off, my jostled body curling down into a corner between seat and cockpit as I slip away into a deep sleep.

I dream of Penelope again. And again, she's in bed. This bed is different, though. A sea of rich black satin, her blonde hair splayed across it like a spill of sunshine, her limbs tangled in the sheets. She feels her own bare breasts, cupping them, squeezing them, pinching the nipples until they've become hard. She's beside herself, rubbing her thighs together, luxuriating in the sexiness of her own body and arousal. She lets out a noise that's half laugh, half squeal of sheer, uninhibited delight, bites her lip and sighs, arching her neck back. Then a pale, taloned hand reaches around that neck, pulls her close so the

Steward can sink his fangs into her throat. She gasps, eyes fluttering as the blood wells around those penetrating fangs, drips in braiding rivulets down her pale flesh, and she creeps a hand down between her legs and begins to pleasure herself, moaning and writhing, as the Steward sucks from her. But he's not done. He has more hunger to satisfy, more love to give. He pulls away with a sigh, blood dribbling from his lips and the tips of his fangs, and turns onto his other side in the bed. Because I'm there, too, beside him, also naked. He bites my neck now, sliding his fangs deep into the silvery scars Evangeline left on me. I do not shrink away, do not scream. I treat this like a blessing. I arch my neck to welcome him, lips parting in a shuddering moan as I begin to touch myself, too, Penelope cuddling up against the Steward's back and kissing his shoulder as she watches me, open-mouthed, hips grinding, her hand working feverishly between her legs as she lets out little rapturous sounds of horniness, exultant in the sharing of her lover. She meets my eyes, and the two of us smile and kiss his pale, flat chest, his stomach, and drift down lower, his hands tangling in our hair as his eyelids slide shut, a beatific smile widening his blood-smeared mouth . . .

"Baby."

I jolt awake, my body flushed with unclean shame, and realize to my horror that I'm wet.

No. That wasn't me. That couldn't have been my wants, my desires. That was him. Him communicating to me through dreams, the same way he did with Penelope. Him trying to seduce me.

Nothing—nothing at all—to do with me.

"Baby?"

I jerk to see Redfearn watching me, a furrow between his brows. Guilt flames into my cheeks and I push myself upright in my seat, straightening my skirt. "Y-Yes?"

Redfearn's gaze lingers on me, and for a moment I have the horrible suspicion he somehow knows what I'd been dreaming. I look back at him with all the innocence I can muster.

Then he looks out through the cracked windshield of the tender. "We're here."

We've reached the northern tip of Hainan with its range of volcanoes. But not just Hainan. There's an island off its coast, perhaps seven kilometers long. Jungle-green and wild, with the black cone of a volcano dominating it. And this volcano is active. Smoke rises from it in a rank black pillar into the sky, turning everything to the west into a glowering dusk. Here and there, it spews up lumps of twisted molten rock that drop into the sea like flaming meteors. And all around it, cracks and fissures glow, erupting with gouts of lava that flow in hissing rivers into the sea in a haze of hot steam and sulfuric acid clouds.

My lips part. "*Where fire meets the sea,*" I whisper.

Redfearn frowns at me. "What's that?"

"I—I remember now," I say with a chill. "This is where he was going to take me on our anniversary, before—"

Sunlight bounces off glass and fiberglass, and I stiffen in my seat. Somehow, impossibly, it's there. That old Sunseeker Predator yacht is bobbing off the coast of that rugged isle, waiting for me. He's here. Come to make me his bride again. Come to consummate his wedding night.

Horror blurs the world gray.

And when I blink again, that cruiser yacht is gone. Just the glare of light off the sea. Just a hallucination. An omen.

I swallow and finish: "It's where we were going to get properly married."

Red patches have appeared in Redfearn's cheeks. I hear his teeth grind as he takes in that volcanic island, his knuckles whitening on the wheel. He lets out a low, bitter chuckle. "Of course it is."

I tangle my fingers in his hair at the back of his head, give him a long, sympathetic look when he meets my gaze. He winces a smile. "Well," he gruffs. "I suppose we better find this forge." He eyes that island in its wrack of volcanic smog, inclines his head at the cone. "Do you think that's it?"

I retrieve a pair of binoculars from the dash, lift them to my face. Nothing but jungly slopes, sections of black lava sand deposited with a woven mat of weeds and the bones of fish and seabirds. And then I see it: a break in the coastline, a narrow channel of water that winds between those lava-dripping cliffs and into the darkness inside that volcano.

"Yes," I say, lowering the binoculars. "I think you're right."

Nodding, Redfearn turns on the tender's engines again, scans the horizon one last time to make sure we're not being followed. Then he eases us forward, taking us across the waves and into the Forge of the Bloodsmith.

TWENTY-ONE

The first thing I notice is the heat.

It emanates from the lava flowing in waterfalls of incandescent sludge into the sea, wafts out of the cleft that leads inside the volcano. It's everywhere, practically radiating from the island.

And then there's the smell.

A hot, gritty wind whips along the coast, blowing wisps of white steam clouds our way. The acrid smell of sulfur. I cough, eyes stinging, and Redfearn hands me a handkerchief. "Here. It's toxic gas. From the hydrochloric acid. Don't breathe it in."

I shake my head as I press the handkerchief over my nose and mouth. "Only a vampire would think to live here."

And only an idiot would pay a visit.

"Have you heard anything about this Bloodsmith?" I ask.

Redfearn's mouth thins. "Only what Adrian has mentioned in passing. That they call him the Father of Familiars. And that he is old. Very old. It's said Volok entrusted him with his duty at the founding of their yacht club."

As if hearing this, it floats back to us from far, far within. The echo of a sharp, metallic ringing: *cling*, *cling*, *cling*.

As if the smith were summoning us.

A shudder prickles down my spine. I glance at Redfearn.

Swallowing, he slows the tender as he guides us inside the volcano.

Shadows fall over us as we slip between those cliffs. The cleft rears up for hundreds of feet, a jagged crack in the verdant slopes of the mountain. And for a moment, all is darkness.

Redfearn flips a switch for the boat sidelights, and strips of red and green LED lights on the port and starboard hull pulse on. That bicolored glow illuminates walls of rock sliding past, a body of dark water lapping inside what sounds like a vast cavern: the heart of the volcano.

And then, ahead, we see another glow.

This one's a sooty orange, like the flame-filled breast of a dragon. It's lava glowing under the surface of the lake in here. Many columns of pillow lava extruding up from vents deep below, blistering with fissures of molten light before they cool into blocks of black basaltic rock, making the water bubble and give off steam. And the glow is not just from lava. On the far side of the lake, on a shore of black rock, is the forge. It's a rotund behemoth of iron, its open maw a blurry glaze of heat sending up a column of smoke through the hollow peak of the volcano, up, and up, and up into a distant patch of blue sky.

My skin goes rough and hard with gooseflesh.

So this is the Forge of the Bloodsmith.

Another boat floats at a jetty by the lakeshore: a sleek black trimaran with a flat deck over its three hulls and a single black sail, making me think of a sinister manta ray. Farther beyond, in the shadows dappled with pale light from the topside world, the shape of another boat. This one older. Much older. A twin-masted rig lying half-keeled over in a stand of stalagmites, its hull staved in, its lolling rags of sail blackened with soot. Perhaps from when the Bloodsmith first foundered here in some storm and took up his trade. It must have been here for hundreds of years, might be for hundreds more.

Redfearn puts us in at the jetty beside the trimaran.

I jump out with the bow line and tie us off, my nose wrinkling. The sulfurous rotten egg smell is stronger in here, making me gag. I have to bend over for a moment, hands on knees, and realize I'm staring at a pale gleam of skull, the bones of victims strewn along the shoreline in a tidewrack of death. The Bloodsmith must use the trimaran to go out hunting. This is the den of a beast.

It's there, shivering and trembling with my hands on my knees, that I hear him announce himself.

Cling, cling, cling.

Redfearn, stiffening as he takes my arm, turns with me to see.

He stands at an anvil before the forge's blinding maw, a glistening silhouette pounding out some shape of metal with a hammer. Sparks fly. Scales flake away in bright leaps of light. The scurf bounces in hot cinders around his boots, his shadow flung long across the inland shore. He looks like a figure from an old story in this cavern fanged with the drippings of old molten rock. His hammer falls, the crash and ring of metal echoing everywhere in his underkingdom. He lifts the glowing bar with a pair of tongs, dips it into a slake-trough in a hiss of steam.

When the steam clears enough to reveal his face again, it has lifted to stare at us with glowing red slits of eyes.

Somehow, in all this heat, I grow cold.

A hint of a smile twitches that fierce pale face, and then the Bloodsmith pulls the cooled bar of metal from the slake-trough, frowns and tosses it onto a slag heap. "He said you'd come," he grunts. His voice is as deep as the rumblings of his home. He sets his hammer and tongs on the anvil and approaches, tugging off gauntlet-like gloves. He wears a shiny leather blacksmith's apron over his bare torso, his burly arms smeared with sweat and black streaks of soot. He's built like a mountain.

He wipes sweat from the shaved dome of his head, extends his other hand. "Contract."

With trembling fingers, I pull the papers from my skirt pocket and hand them to him.

He squints at the fine print in the dull glow of the forge, finds it easier to parse the red blotch of my blood seal at the bottom. "The Steward is your master?"

I can feel Redfearn's eyes on me, but can't make myself look at him. "Yes."

"When did he enlist your services?"

I draw a blank, not knowing how to answer that. Then I think of the Steward proposing to me here in China. "Many years ago."

"Where is his mark on you?"

Where did he not leave his mark on me?

I know he wants an answer, though. I give him a lie and indicate the fang mark scars on my neck.

The Bloodsmith grunts, satisfied, and tucks the folded-up contract into an apron pocket as he turns away.

He goes up to a benchtop molding press and flips a switch to heat its steel plates, places round casino chip blanks into its mold cups, then gold inlays into the recesses in the middle of the blanks. He punches a green button and the ram lowers onto the die. When it rises again, the casino chips have been compressed and stamped, the gold embedded into the chips in the signature eyeteeth design of *The Palace of the Fang*. He repeats this process on the other side, then takes out the newly molded chips one by one and places them in a rack, presents the rack to Redfearn. "Careful," he grunts. "Still warm."

The captain and I look at each other, tentative joy filling our faces. We have them. We have the chips. We can enter the palace now.

We have a chance of getting Penelope back.

But doubt rushes in. Surely it can't be as easy as that. Surely there's another reason for Mr. Colding to bring me here. There must be something worse to come.

And it does.

"The silver," the Bloodsmith grunts, staring at me.

I glance at Redfearn, back at the smith. "The what?"

"You didn't bring it?" The old vampire's eyes hood. "The silver. Five grams. The Steward not tell you?"

Cold dread blossoms in my gut.

"You need a ring. To become his familiar. A symbol of you cleaving yourself to him." He inclines the great dome of his head, indicating the necklace hanging from my neck that Redfearn gave me. "That should do."

My stomach drops. I take a step back, instinctively clutching the half-moon pendant. "*No.*"

The Bloodsmith shrugs his massive shoulders. "Then you cannot become Steward's familiar." He reaches for the casino chips—

"Wait!"

Redfearn holds the chips to his chest, looks at me. An anguished determination there.

I shake my head, my heart twisting. "No . . ."

"It's okay," he soothes, though his face says it isn't. "It's all right. It's the only way."

It was the only way, wasn't it? Because the Steward made sure it was. He saw the necklace at our meetup on the open sea, must have known Redfearn had given it to me.

He knew what it would mean—what damage it would cause—to turn Redfearn's necklace into his ring of ownership over me. He knew what it would symbolize.

Everything he touches is corrupted.

"I hate him," I say in a vehement whisper. "God, I hate him."

"Then do it," Redfearn growls, his face ferocious in the light from the forge. "So we can be rid of him."

Teeth clenched, I unclasp the necklace with shaking fingers, hold it out to the Bloodsmith. I will not look at him.

He takes it.

He wastes no time. He drops the necklace into a crucible, grips the crucible with tongs and places it in the coals of the roaring forge. Before long the crucible turns orange, so hot it seems to glow from within, and I watch with stinging eyes as that necklace with its half-moon begins to melt into a bubbling, mercurial sludge.

Redfearn steps close to wrap an arm around me, kiss my temple. *You'll always be my sailor moon*, that kiss says.

I stare on, burning this into my brain so I never forget.

This is what he does.

The Bloodsmith grips the crucible with the tongs again and pulls it out of the flames, walks it over to an iron mold and pours the molten silver into its hole. The silver looks like a spill of lava, like a bubbling of liquid sun. He sets the fire-red crucible aside and waits.

I catch Redfearn glancing at his watch. Three hours until sunset.

We don't have time for this.

At last, the Bloodsmith picks up the tongs again, uses them to bang down the iron hoop keeping the mold together, and the mold's two halves topple back to reveal the silver that now lies between them. It's been cast into a ring.

My stomach twists at the sight.

The Bloodsmith retrieves the band with the tongs and quenches it in the slake-trough in a spitting hiss of water, drops it onto the anvil. Then the filing and sanding, polishing the dulled silver until it's regained its shine, his arms blurring and weaving so that they're in many places at once, as if in a trance of some kind of vampire magic. I don't know how long he works; time seems to slow, become strange. Finally, he holds the ring up to the light to eye its perfection.

Then he's returning.

He asks for my hand, and I give it. He turns it over so my palm is exposed, flicks a talon across it to unseam my skin.

I flinch.

He tips my hand so the blood drips into a metal pan he's produced from somewhere.

Then he's turned away, his mountainlike shoulders bowed over the anvil once more, engaged in some secret work.

I wrap the handkerchief Redfearn gave me around my hand and glance at the captain. Neither of us like where this is going.

It's not long before the old nightwalker returns, and I know why he is called the Bloodsmith.

He holds the ring in one giant palm, the gem perched on its setting a glazed blood stone. My blood.

He bids me kneel.

Redfearn takes a step forward, a vein pulsing on his brow. The Bloodsmith swivels his head at him and he rocks to a stop, swallows hard.

I sink to my knees.

The Bloodsmith looks down at me with his glowing red eyes, his backdrop the forge. It outlines his shadowy body in golden light, picking out the hairs on his massive forearms, dancing on the sweaty, soot-stained curves of biceps as big as my head.

He speaks.

"Do you swear to serve your Master in both sun and dark, until his end or yours?"

The rock floor of the volcano is cutting into my knees, but I don't care. I tell myself I deserve this pain.

This is the only altar I deserve.

I have to take a moment to clear my throat before I speak. "I do."

"Do you swear to serve him loyally, whether that be the giving or taking of blood, even if it be your life?"

The blood thumps in my ears. I nod, as if that will shake loose the words. "I do."

"Do you swear to forsake all other vows of matrimony and always be his?"

My heart stumbles as I glance at Redfearn waiting in the shadows like an objecting groomsman. His face twists, his shoulders trembling as he looks at me with tortured eyes: *Don't do it.*

And Mr. Colding's voice now, answering from the past. (*You're* mine. *Forever.*)

The Bloodsmith frowns and repeats his question.

(*Forever.*)

I shake my head, my eyes burning, and not from the heat of that accursed forge.

I close them.

"I do," I whisper, feeling something cold trace down my cheek.

Then I feel my hand being taken, cool metal being slid onto my ring finger.

"Rise, familiar of the Steward."

My knees are shaking when I stand, and the world veers. I feel faint. But Redfearn is at my side, taking my arm, leading me away. I cannot bear to look at the obscenity on my hand.

"One more thing."

We freeze.

The Bloodsmith marches to a far wall hung with all manner of tools for metalworking. There's something on a workbench there. He returns with it, holding it in front of him as if afraid to sully it with his grimy self.

He holds it out to me. "A gift from the Steward."

It's a box, its virgin whiteness blinding in this hole of misery. I know what's inside it. I lift the lid anyway.

There's a bridal gown carefully folded within, the extravagance of its lace downright sickening.

So, I think. *I ended up getting married to Mr. Colding here, after all.*

The Bloodsmith's teeth show in a razorous smile. "Congratulations, Mrs. Colding."

TWENTY-TWO

Redfearn fumes as he pilots the amphibious tender out of the Forge of the Bloodsmith.

He glances at that white box in my lap, at the hideous blood ring on my hand, and knuckles the steering wheel until his bones show through his skin. "That motherfucker."

I don't say anything. I sit in the passenger seat beside him, feeling as if my stomach has been poured full of lead.

"The gall. The fucking gall."

"He didn't like it that we were the ones to propose the gambling," I murmur. "He had to feel in control again."

Redfearn's smile is carnivorous. "Oh, he's gonna get it. He's gonna get it."

I look over at him, touch his arm. "This doesn't change anything. I still belong to you."

"Do you?" he scoffs, letting out a harsh laugh. "Because it doesn't feel like it anymore."

My chest clenches painfully, as if I've been stabbed there. "Why would you say that?"

"I don't know," he shrugs, a wild recklessness in his voice now. "I feel as if this fucker's everywhere. Digging his fingers into you. Getting between us."

I take a moment to comport myself, push down a rising panic. "Well," I say carefully, "what *would* make you feel that I belong to—"

I don't finish the sentence. Redfearn lets go of the wheel and grabs my face with both hands, bruises my mouth with a ferocious kiss. The tender stutters to a stop and we bob on the chop.

I pull away, panting, alarmed and heated. "Redfearn, we only have a few hours until sunset. We don't have ti—"

He swipes the box out of my lap and it goes flying, lid bouncing away, folds of white lace exploding out. He pins me back into the seat with his crushing weight, his mouth on mine, greedy and devouring, sucking on my bottom lip, my knees spread on either side of him. My body goes limp with a heated passivity. "Mmph, wait—" I gasp.

He doesn't care. He drags me out of the seat and then I'm on my back, lace and tulle under me, my breath coming in hitching gasps. I push at Redfearn's chest, but his ravenous persistence is dumping heat into me, making me tingle all over with dizzying arousal. Taking me now, taking me here, on the wedding dress Mr. Colding gave me, is him reclaiming me, I know. Marking me as his. A slippery deviancy clutches me as I watch him. His mouth dips to my cleavage, then down my belly and under my skirt, and I put my hand on his head, not sure if I'm pushing him away or keeping him there. I'm already dangerously wet.

"Fuck," I whisper.

His hands cup my ass, gripping my panties. He catches them in his teeth and tugs them aside, and then his mouth is on me, making me stiffen and gasp. "Redfearn . . ."

But he doesn't stop. He kisses and sucks and licks, his tongue swirling, and my eyes roll back into my head as I run a hand down my face, fingers catching on my bottom lip and pulling it, traveling farther down and over the swell of my breast to touch and squeeze it through my yachtie polo. "Redfearn," I whisper, his name becoming a chant. "Redfearn . . ."

He can't take it anymore. He has to have me. He lifts his head out from under my skirt and tugs at his belt buckle, and I'm helping him, unzipping his khaki shorts, pulling them down, pulling at his black boxer briefs, and then he's holding himself, guiding himself inside me, and I'm pulling him down on top of me. He doesn't want my help. He pins my hands over my head and rolls his hips, grinding himself all the way in, driving a sharp gasp out me. And then he's pumping into me, hard and angry and possessive, his breaths coming rough and short. The power of it, the need of it, makes my hands curl into fists, my legs wrap around him, pulling him deeper.

"Fuck me, baby," I whimper, urging him on. "Fuck me . . ."

He obliges, bracing himself over me so he can pound into me, making my breasts bounce, and I bite my lip, a helpless moan escaping my lips. The pleasure sends me gasping and bowing up, my brow resting against his, and we both look down to watch him going in and out of me.

"Oh shit," I whisper, lips parted, and drop my head back.

It's too much. It's overwhelming. I can't remember ever being taken like this. I can't remember ever being wanted like this.

It's driving me mad.

But something's off. Something's wrong. I'm so turned on, so wet, I should be coming by now. I am almost out of my mind with arousal. But it's not happening.

I am thinking of my dream.

It flashes into my head. The Steward's teeth sinking into my neck, my lips parting with a moan. My body writhing, breasts heaving. My hand stealing between my legs to do its sly, dirty work.

No.

I shake this away with a toss of disgust, bringing myself back to Redfearn. To us.

I wriggle my wrists free and pull him to me, moaning into his mouth.

(I moan in the dream.)

I squirm and writhe, feeling my breast.

(I feel my breast.)

I shut my eyes, shake my head.

(I toss and turn, eyes shut in rapture.)

A frantic desperation fills me. I whisper hotly into Redfearn's ear. "I want it, baby."

He stiffens, pulls back to give me a questioning look.

"I want it," I say again, tugging at him, imploring him, voice low with need. "Come inside me. Make me yours."

Redfearn's eyes darken with desire. He dips his head to seal my mouth with his, and he begins to pound into me again, making my whole body rock up and down on our bower of bridal tulle. I tug at his back, nails digging into flesh. "Yes," I moan. "Yes, baby. Give it to me."

Make me forget.

Drive these thoughts away.

Redfearn's thrusts quicken, faster and faster, and then his muscles go rigid under my hands and he's groaning, crying out, throbbing rhythmically inside me. And then he's coming.

The feel of him filling me up—the explosion of sticky wetness, turning me soft and mushy and devoted in his arms—is almost overwhelming.

This, I think. *This surely must do it.*

But the wave of pleasure crests, teeters—and it hasn't happened. I haven't come for him.

A sudden fear grips me. A fear of what this means.

I can't have that.

"Bite me," I whisper.

Redfearn lifts his head, panting, brows drawn in confusion. "What?"

I touch my fingers to my neck, the silver fang-mark scars there. "Bite me."

His face slackens. "Are you—you sure?"

"Mmhmm." I nod, desperate, writhing under him, still impaled and trembling.

He sees the need in my eyes, the animal ferocity, and stops second-guessing it. He drops his head to my neck, incisors pricked against the scars, and presses down, hard.

I gasp, a fluttering thrill tightening my stomach. There's the flash of Evangeline's face in my mind, as horrible as a nightmare, and I expect a tumble of fear and pain, an incapacitating panic. But I don't.

All I feel is pleasure.

Then I'm lifting my hips to grind myself on Redfearn's still-hard cock inside me, my hand slipping between my legs to feverishly pleasure myself. *(I pleasure myself).* I moan, lips parted, trembling in the grip of Redfearn's jaws, and then that tingling is coiling tighter and tighter and my stomach flattens, my thighs clamp, my body rocking back as the ecstasy blazes through me, brought to an unbearable height by those paralyzing jaws on my neck.

(The Steward's jaws on my neck, making me shudder and moan.)

Shame floods through my body, mixing with all that pleasure, turning it sour, corrupted, wrong, and I cover my face with my hands, suck in a rattling wail of breath.

Redfearn freezes.

"Hey," he says, eyes round. "What is it?"

I hiccup sobs, shoulders shaking, barely able to get out the words. "What's happening to me?" I cry. "What's wrong with me?"

Redfearn, horrified, tries to pull my hands away from my face. "Hey. It's okay. You did nothing wrong."

I wrap my arms around his neck and pull him to me. He holds me. "What is it?" he says, voice low, soothing, patient. "You can tell me."

"He—he—he's been sending me dreams," I choke, unable to look at him. "They're—foul. *Carnal.*"

Redfearn stiffens.

I open my eyes to look at him. His face is scarily pale.

I hold it in my hands. "It was nothing," I assure him, stomach plunging in terror. "That wasn't—I don't love him. It's a trauma bond. It's like an addiction. He's trying to pull me back into it—"

"Hey," he says, wiping the tears from my cheeks. "It's okay. I'm not mad. I know it's not you."

I stare into his eyes, searching them for confirmation. That he's not judging me. That I haven't lost him. Haven't driven him away.

He puts a hand over mine, gives me a gentle smile.

It makes the tears well up in my eyes again, and I bury myself in his neck. "He's ruining everything," I sob. "We should—we should be *happy.*"

He holds me for a long time, stroking the taut hair of my bun. "I love you," he whispers, over and over, accepting everything about me. "I love you. We are happy."

After some time, my trembling stops. I take in deep, exhausted, cleansing breaths, curl my fingers into his shirt. "You're right," I whisper, voice hard as stone. "We have to destroy him." When I pull back to look at him, I offer a wan smile. "I have an idea. It's risky, but it just might work."

He raises a brow. "Do tell."

I lean to whisper into his ear, as if afraid the very wind would overhear it, report back to the Steward.

Redfearn's eyes go wide.

I kiss his cheek.

We slowly sit up all the way, disentangle from each other. We smile, mussed and rumpled like teenagers, the wedding dress a wrinkled mess under us. I look around for my panties, find Redfearn's hooked them up by a finger, and I laugh and take them, slip them on.

I stand, straightening my skirt, patting my hair, and look about.

We didn't get far from the Forge of the Bloodsmith. A pathetically short distance, really. We bob maybe a quarter mile off its coast, having drifted a few hundred feet or so during our—*intermission.*

The island is lush and stark in the afternoon light, the sea chipped gold. Something on it flashes. Something approaching.

It's a boat.

It's that Sunseeker Predator yacht again. It's found us. *He's* found us.

No, I remind myself. *Just an hallucination. That boat is back in Florida, remember? It's in your head.*

Then one of the passengers stands from its deck, lifts an assault rifle to its shoulder, and fires.

TWENTY-THREE

The salvo rackets across the amphibious tender, punching holes into it—*thunk thunk thunk*—and bits of fiberglass go flying as Redfearn grunts and drags me down. Lying between the twin bench seating, I blink. My ears are ringing, my head blank with the adrenaline surge of shock. And there's—red. Red freckling the seating, flung onto the glass windscreen behind us, on my arms and polo. It's blood. But not mine—not mine—

I look up from my trembling hands. Redfearn lies with his head and shoulder propped against a bench, teeth gritted, a hand slapped over his left arm. Blood oozes between his fingers.

My stomach plunges. My jaw hangs. I move toward him, hands outstretched, aching with fear and tender love. "Redfearn—"

"It's okay," he grunts. "Just grazed me. I'll be fine."

"But—"

"How was my aim, captain?" a lazy voice drawls. "Stings, I hope?"

My skin chills. Redfearn's eyes swivel to me. I crouch on my knees, lift my head just high enough to peer over the tender's portside gunwale.

That other boat has drifted up, maybe five meters off. But it's no Sunseeker Predator yacht. It's a speedboat. A vicious-looking thing, lean and black with red accents, a hardtop shade over the cockpit to shield its passengers from the sun. And they need shielding, judging from their pale skin and glowing eyes, the rows of needle fangs flashing out of the gloom.

One of them rests the stock of his assault rifle on his hip. He's broad, with the belly of a glutton barely constrained by a sharp black suit, his silver-streaked hair drawn back in a manbun. A manbun like—

"I am Hong, owner of *The Palace of the Fang*. You killed my son, Hong-Li. I don't know which one of you did it, but as that chief stew bitch is the Steward's familiar, Captain Redfearn will pay the price in his heart's blood."

Redfearn and I lock eyes. My pulse rises, stoppering my ears, beating dull and hard in my skull.

They found us.

Redfearn points at the weapon cases, and I drag them over as Hong continues speaking. "Will you make it easy?" Engines purr as his speedboat slowly circles us, drawing closer, closer. "If you give yourself up, captain, I promise I won't enjoy myself with the familiar."

We unlatch the weapons cases and lift the lids. Fitted into the luxurious foam lining are a pair of AR-15s.

We get to work.

"Unfortunately, I can't make any promises to you. I'm going to take my time draining you. There's no avoiding that."

Following Redfearn's lead, I lift out my rifle, press-check the top round in the ammo magazine and slap it into the barrel, do a push-pull check on the mag and hit the bolt release to chamber the first round. Then I lift my head over the gunwale again.

A second speedboat is approaching. And it's close. It'll be here in less than thirty seconds.

That's what Hong has been doing. Distracting us to buy time for that other boat to move into position and pincer us. Pin us down with their guns while one of them boards us and takes Redfearn.

We need to move. Now.

I look at Redfearn, lift two fingers. He understands, tucks the butt of his AR-15 into his shoulder. Nods.

As one, we both rise up and fire.

The assault rifles blaze coronas of light, pocking up the boat's hull and cratering its glass with white spiderwebs. I aim for Hong, one eye shut, my limbs locked in a cool, hard rage. That sonofabitch can burn in hell for shooting my man.

I clip his ear, splashing the air red and leaving his earlobe hanging by a few gutty strings of flesh. The pain spins him back into the cockpit, cursing in Cantonese. The others dive down, not having expected us to be armed, and the pilot throttles the thrusters, lurching the speedboat away in a deep flume of water.

Redfearn wastes no time. He tosses his rifle onto the passenger seat and slides behind the wheel, revving our tender away.

"Fucking whore!" Hong roars behind us, his hand clapped to his ear. "You shot me! You fucking shot my ear off! You fucking fucks! I'll fucking *kill you!*"

I seat myself on one of the twin benches and cast my gaze astern. Hong's boat is cutting a wide arc through the water to come up on our tail again. But that other boat has bombed straight for us, skipping across the waves in great roaring surges that lift its hull into the air. In no less than a few seconds it's bearing down on us, its momentum already too fast for us to outrun, aiming to do a pass on our port side. I brace my AR-15 against my shoulder, sight through its scope with its red dot reticle. One of those pale passengers hangs over the gunwale of the boat with a machine gun and starts firing at our twin outboard engines, aiming to put us dead in the water. I aim that red dot dead center in his chest and squeeze off a short burst that knocks him off the speedboat into the frothing waves, leaving him to scream, thrashing and smoking, as the sun strikes his flesh.

I don't stop shooting. Another is popping off a pistol at Redfearn, smacking holes into the windshield, the cockpit exploding with sparks as if fried by a high-voltage wire. Redfearn ducks, cursing and shielding his head, and rage zings up my spine. I won't have any of that.

That's my man. That's the man I love.

I slowly swivel, following the path of the speedboat, the AR-15 kicking back into my shoulder as I fire and fire, one eye squinted, jaw clenched and cheeks trembling from the force, and blast that would-be assassin back into the speedboat as if he's been kicked by a horse.

Then the boat has roared past in a whine of engines and blast of spray, its whole side shredded and shiny with bullet holes, and one of its passengers has leapt into the tender and on top of me.

The impact bounces my head hard off the gunwale and I see stars. For a moment, I can't comprehend what's happened. Our tender is open to the sun. One of them would never do this—

Then I see that this one wears a heavy suit with black gloves, a black ski mask over his head like a bank robber, eyes and bared fangs flashing out of the cutouts.

He slaps the AR-15 out of my hands with contemptuous ease and I hear it splash overboard. His backhanded swipe knocks me into the floor of the boat, my ears ringing again.

Then he starts for Redfearn, who in all the roar of the tender's high speed hasn't noticed there's an intruder aboard.

I blink, seeing double, and grab at the vampire's ankle. "Redfearn!" I gasp.

The captain doesn't hear. The intruder shakes me off, his shoe clipping me in the face, and keeps walking, balancing himself on the twin benches as he goes.

When I look up again, the vampire is right behind Redfearn, reaching for his neck—

My heart drops. *"REDFEARN!"*

This time, the captain hears. He whirls, his face paling as he sees the intruder looming over him.

Then his hand blurs.

He pulls out his Heckler & Koch P30, but the intruder seizes his wrist, bashes it against the cockpit console and sends the pistol flying.

That's as far as he gets.

Because I'm up, charging down the aisle, and the vampire only has time to freeze, mouth hanging in stupid surprise, before I've thudded a bare foot into his chest, pinning him with a crash against the console. My skirt rides up, revealing that push dagger strapped to my thigh.

I unsheathe it with one hard pull and slash it across the thing's throat.

Blood leaps in a lurid streak across the windshield. There's a gurgle and the vampire's neck flops back, blood sheeting down the front of his suit.

I lean in, nostrils flared. "Don't touch my man."

And hooking a hand under one of the vampire's legs, I pitch him overboard, his body instantly lost in the spray behind us.

Redfearn blinks at me, mouth hanging, quivering droplets of blood clinging to his lashes. He looks as if he's never seen me before.

I sheathe my dagger, grab up Redfearn's AR-15 and seat myself beside him. I flop a hand. "We going?"

Redfearn's face breaks into a helpless, admiring snort of a smile.

Then his eyes widen as his gaze strays behind us, and he revs the tender again.

I turn to look.

Hong's boat is barreling down on us, plowing up white leaps of foam.

When I look ahead again, we're gunning straight for the island's cliffs.

"What are you doing?" I ask, brow raised as we careen closer and closer toward all that soaring, water-pounded rock.

"Losing them," Redfearn growls, and yanks the wheel.

The amphibious tender tilts hard into the turn, lifting my side into the air until we're parallel to the cliffs, skipping along in its shadow. We're close. Too close. So near the fissure vents above, we're within striking distance of those lava bombs. They flame down out of the sky around us, molten meteors that crash hissing into the sea. Redfearn jerks hard on the wheel to avoid them, weaving through their smoking paths, their sizzling splashes erupting like whale spouts around us.

"Redfearn," I breathe, hands braced on the dash.

"Just hold on."

Hong is gaining on us, the whine of his speedboat rising to a monstrous pitch. He levels his assault rifle over the cockpit windshield, grinning wide. He's only three meters off. From this distance, he can't miss.

"Redfearn!" I shout, gripping his arm.

And a lava bomb explodes onto the foredeck of Hong's boat.

It punches a blackened hole through it the size of a sewer grate, splattering the speedboat with globs of pulsing, molten muck. The force of the impact smacks the bow of the boat into the sea. It catches and in the blink of an eye the boat's tumbled into a terrifying death roll, shedding bodies and bits of mangled metal before it lands on its hull again, half-destroyed and smoking.

Leaving only the second boat in pursuit.

And Redfearn can't shake it.

They hang on our tail, their pilot far more skilled than Hong's. And they're still armed. Bullets rat-a-tat around us, red-hot metal zipping past our ears to stitch lines of splashes across the water.

"Fuck!" Redfearn growls, hunching into his shoulders, and stills as he looks ahead.

We're coming across the lava rivers flowing over the cliffs into the sea, hissing up billowing clouds of toxic gas. Farther on, those clouds get denser, turning into an impenetrable haze.

Redfearn tightens his grip on the wheel and steers straight for it.

"You *do* remember that gas is poisonous, right?" I shout over the wind and whine of the engines.

"I remember," Redfearn growls, dodging a glowing meteor of half-molten rock.

"So this is another one of those times that I have to trust you?"

Redfearn grins his dangerous, rakish grin. "We have a canopy back there. I want you to put it up and get inside."

A canopy? No we—

But we do. I twist around to see that there are retractable panels sheathed into the gunwales. *You must be joking. What* doesn't *this tender have?* I stumble over to the starboard one, grasp its edge with both hands and rock it upward. It swings up surprisingly easily and clicks in place, forming half a cabin shell, leaving only the cockpit outside of it. Stumbling to port, I grab the other half and rock it halfway out of its sheath, turn to Redfearn.

"Get in," he orders. "I'll be right behind you."

I hop in. Through the gap in the panels astern, that speedboat from *The Palace of the Fang* can be seen. It looks like an angel of death, spitting fire that tears up our aft, bullets sparking and ricocheting off the casings of our engines, making one smoke.

"Redfearn!"

"Here goes nothing." Redfearn throttles us dead toward the looming wall of gas and then pulls the kill switch, killing the engines. He dives through the gap in the canopy and I rock it closed, sealing us in just as we whip into the cloud bank.

It's as if we've entered the infernal regions. All is smoke, the hiss of sizzling elements. Particles of lava glass tick against the window panes, those white clouds of gas so thick we can see no more than a meter beyond us. Our momentum quickly dies and we rock to a crawl, water lapping against the tender's hull.

And then our pursuers roar past us in the gloom.

If they see us, it's too late. They whip past, having no time to avoid the next waterfall of lava. It leaves a streak of gurgling gloop as viscous as honey along their boat, that heavy, flaming sludge collapsing their roof, softening and sagging in their windshield. Horrified screams pierce the netherworld, and the boat veers off, careening into the vague shapes of coastal rocks. A mushroom of boiling flame pulses in the gloom.

And then wisps of steam part and we're floating out of that noxious cloudbank, as calm and innocent as a couple on a pleasure cruise.

We blink at each other, crouched and bodies stiff, our breaths still uneven. Then we rouse ourselves and crack the pop-up canopy, just a hair's breadth, ready to shut it again at any hint of acid on the wind. But all we smell is the sea, clean and pure and fresh in our nostrils. Rocking one half of the canopy all the way back into its gunwale, we stagger out into the open. The world shines, deceiving in its serenity. The dome of sky above is as blue as a robin's egg.

Redfearn and I look at each other, not knowing how we did that. Not knowing what we just went through. We're too stunned to even smile.

Then, intruding into that peaceful silence like a clap of thunder: a faint ringtone, a vibrating in my skirt pocket.

Someone's calling my phone.

Redfearn and I lock eyes.

I pull out the phone and check the caller ID: THE STEWARD.

My chest is suddenly too tight for my heart. My pulse knocks in my temples. Flicking a glance at Redfearn, I answer the call.

"Hello?"

But the voice that pours into my ears isn't my husband's. This one's soft, shaky, and full of terror. "Mrs. Colding? Is that you?"

I fly my eyes to Redfearn. I don't even have time to tell him, because he's snatched the phone from me. "Pen?" he says, his voice hoarse.

"Daddy." The word is a quavery, held-back sob. "I don't have much time. He doesn't know I have his phone—"

Redfearn paces, his shoulders high, a wild, distraught look in his eyes. "Are you okay?"

Penelope sucks in a harsh breath, on the verge of a breakdown. "It's like I woke from a dream. He—he bit me again, and I was put back under. But now—now it's different. He doesn't have the same power over me. And I can see now that he's—that I—" Her voice catches and goes quiet suddenly, as if she's held a hand to her mouth. "I'm so sorry, Dad. I made a huge mistake. I didn't want to leave you—"

"It's okay." Redfearn shuts his eyes, a muscle flaring in his jaw, and a thick feeling rises in my throat. I touch his arm. "Can you get away?"

A sniffling now, Penelope trying to pull herself together. "No. This is the only time I've left his sight. He has body guards posted outside the door—"

"You're at the casino?"

"Yes."

Redfearn nods. "Just hang in there. I have a plan. Everything will be okay—"

But there's a taut silence on the other end of the line. Then, the two words soft and petrified: "He's coming."

My flesh crawls along my spine.

Very faint, footsteps can be heard on the phone. Then another voice, lilting, gently scolding. "There you are, my sweet." The words squirm themselves out of the tiny speakers and wrap themselves around my throat. "How naughty you've been . . ."

Redfearn pales. Then he grips the phone tightly to his ear. "Sweetheart, listen to me. I'm coming for you. Do you hear? I swear on my soul I'll get you back—"

"I love you, Daddy—"

Tears spring to Redfearn's eyes. "Pen!"

But the line goes dead.

Redfearn stands there staring at the black screen, breath ragged, shoulders heaving. Then he lifts his reddened eyes to me. The raw grief there is like a stab in my guts.

Then he catches sight of the sun over my shoulder, and his jaw clamps.

He checks his watch: two hours until sunset. *The Palace of the Fang* is two hours away.

He lifts his face to me, his expression as hard as granite. "Let's go."

TWENTY-FOUR

The amphibious tender blasts over the sea toward the boiling sun hanging over the horizon.

We waited to leave only long enough for me to do a hasty patch-up job on Redfearn's arm. I found a first aid kit in the dash, poured on some disinfectant before sewing up with a needle and thread, my stiches as neat as my folding when turning back cabin sheets. The wound wasn't too deep, but it had bled a good deal, and Redfearn looks pale and tired as he pilots the tender toward *The Palace of the Fang*.

"I can take a turn," I offer, but Redfearn shakes his head.

"I'm the fastest pilot between the two of us. We don't have much time."

I check Redfearn's diving watch gleaming on his wrist as he grips the wheel. An hour until sunset.

I feel the fading light as keenly as a sleeping vampire waiting for the start of night. The sun sinks lower and lower, its blurry disc of molten gold turning red as it nears the sea.

"Do you remember where the palace is?" I ask, my throat dry.

Redfearn grimaces as the tender hits a patch of rough chop. "I'll find it."

The sun kisses the sea, reefs of bloodred cloud drifting before it. Not much time.

We round a curve in the coastline of Southern China, and Redfearn straightens in his seat. "I remember this. We're close. Should only be a few miles now."

That's when we see the group of speedboats break away from a hidden cove, their trajectory curving to intercept us.

My blood runs cold.

Of course. Of course there would be more of them. Lying in wait, ready to ambush us as we neared the palace. Because the Steward would have told them where we were headed.

Redfearn looks at me, both despondency and weary resolve in his face. I nod.

As he throttles the tender, I grab an ammo mag from the weapons case and slap it into the remaining AR-15, hit the bolt release to chamber a round.

A first salvo arcs toward us, glowing tracers that whip over our heads and corkscrew into the water beyond. I rise, prop an arm on the windshield, tuck the AR-15 into my shoulder, and return fire.

I'm lucky. My hail of bullets takes out the nearest pilot and his speedboat crashes into the one beside his, tipping it over and pitching its passengers into the sea.

Redfearn guns it, trying to outstrip the remaining boats before they intercept. We both know that if they cut us off, it's over.

The engines rise to a high, unstable whine, and the one that had been smoking before starts up again.

Another hail of bullets clatter toward us, peppering the side of the tender and ricocheting off its brightwork. Redfearn and I hunch down and wait out the barrage, rise again.

We're nearly there. And the speedboats are only five meters off our port side. The vampires ramp up their fire, the air becoming thick with tracers, a dusk alive with murderous fireflies.

Their lead boat pulls ahead, close enough to shove us aside and out to sea.

Redfearn, jaw clenching, keeps us headed straight, the only way to pass them and keep toward the palace.

We're not going to make it.

I prop an arm on the windshield again and open fire. I don't aim for the boat's passengers; I aim for its engines. Bullets riddle the closest one, slapping a scattering of shiny silver holes into its cowling. Then it sparks and coughs out a stream of black smoke. The boat slows, losing its lead on us, but others pull ahead to take its place.

I aim for the next boat, squeeze the trigger—and the AR-15 jams.

Damn.

I yank out the mag and slap it in again, press the bolt release and squeeze the trigger.

It clicks on nothing.

I toss the AR-15 aside and scan the boats. They're almost within spitting distance now. They're going to cut us off. It's almost sunset and we're not going to make it. It's over.

The nearest boat comes abreast of us, set to ram us off-course.

Despair pours into me.

And a rocket shell streaks past to explode into the enemy boat.

It's like a clap of thunder against our ears. One moment, the boat is there. And then it's gone, blown out of the water in a somersaulting of cooked wreckage. A massive cloud of flame boils upward and Redfearn and I duck our heads as we pass through it, whipping past the other boats toward *The Palace of the Fang*.

I whirl.

The other boats surge past behind us, crossing our wake and missing us by seconds. Only to be met by another party: the skiffs of Chung's men.

My jaw drops. We're in the clear. We have the lead.

We have a chance.

Tracers light up the sea as the two parties of boats engage, the rattle of machine-gun fire echoing across the water. One of the skiffs breaks away to come alongside us. There's a group of men crouched in it, black helmets on their heads, strapped in bulletproof vests and gripping tactical rifles. One of them holds a rocket launcher. He whips black polarized sunglasses off his eyes to look at us, and recognition fills me. It's the black ops veteran. He gives us a small, enigmatic smile behind his goatee. "Thought we'd stay in the area in case you needed help," he calls. "Hope you don't mind."

Redfearn and I glance at each other, blinding elation filling our faces. We're too stunned to speak.

The veteran understands. "We'll do our best to give you some time." He lifts two fingers in casual salute, and then his skiff is peeling away to join the firefight.

I look at Redfearn. He inclines his head.

He ramps up the throttle again.

I watch the skirmish as we forge on. Chung's men are highly trained, precise in their firing. They manage to take out two more boats, a third going up in flames from a warhead from the veteran's rocket launcher. But there's too many boats from *The Palace of the Fang*. Enough for them to keep the skiffs busy while others escape the melee to pursue us again.

Redfearn looks at me. Then throttles up our speed to maximum.

This is a mistake. Our engine coughs, its smoke increasing, turning into a billowing black stream that the following speedboats have to swerve aside to avoid, and our tender slows, the needle of its speedometer creeping back.

I gauge the distance to the palace, seeing that familiar cove ahead with its wall of cliffs and tunnel entrance.

That tunnel that leads to *The Palace of the Fang*. It's maybe two miles off.

The boats of our pursuers are faster. They're going to catch up to us.

And there's only a boiling rim of sun still over the ocean. Almost sunset.

We're not going to make it.

"You can escape, you know," I blurt out. "This is my fault they're after us. You can jump overboard with one of the efoil boards, maybe they won't see you. I can tell them the truth. It was me who killed Pongshu's friends. It's me they want."

Redfearn gives me a sidelong stare, his wave of silver hair whipping in the wind. His eyes sparkle with a rakish light as he grins. "Fat chance, sweetheart."

My heart flutters.

"Besides," he adds, tossing his chin at the efoil boards rocking in the stern with the weapons cases. "I hate those things, remember?"

We grin at each other.

I kiss his cheek, and he cranks up the throttle.

Our smoking engine coughs again as we curve into the bay. The cliff walls there are bathed in the lurid light of sunset. The sun is a slice of orange now over the sea, threatening to disappear entirely. And the speedboats have gained on us. They roar and whine only a few boat lengths off our tail. The vampires have stopped firing now, as they can't in the presence of the other yachts lying at anchor in the bay—the patrons of *The Palace of the Fang*.

The crews of those patrons step out on deck to watch as we carom into the bay like a rocket, skidding up great waves of green seawater as we weave between those white boats, aiming for the craggy coastal rock in the shaded leeward side of the cliffs. The boulder by the tunnel entrance where the boatman waits, ready to grant entrance.

We hardly slow down. We hit twenty, thirty, forty knots. The engine is screaming. It bursts into a shower of sparks and then flame is whipping in the wind behind it like a comet. The boat judders and slows, throwing Redfearn and I into the dash.

I look over my shoulder.

The slice of sun is disappearing in a wavering of heat below the sea.

And the speedboats have caught up.

They flicker through the yachts at anchor, approaching the rock from all sides, trying to cut us off. One of them slides up alongside us. A body leans out, a taloned hand snatching at my hair, and I scream as Redfearn bashes the tender into their boat, forcing them to curve away to avoid colliding with a yacht.

The boulder's straight ahead. Only moments now.

The speedboats converge on it, threatening to block us. Our flaming engine screams, coughing and juddering in its brackets, ready to explode.

And the sun sets, turning the sky crimson—

Just as Redfearn skids our tender right up alongside the boulder in a huge wash of spray and I flip a casino coin through the air, its inlays flashing gold in the dusk.

The boatman catches it.

The speedboats fishtail to a stop around us, bodies rushing to gunwales to board our tender, one or two of them already grabbing Redfearn's shirt—

But the boatman lifts a taloned hand.

The vampires freeze, panting, bared fangs gleaming.

The boatman sweeps them all with a cold gaze. The eyes under his conical straw hat flash, as reflective as a night-hunting predator's. "These two have given fare. They are under protection of the palace now."

The vampires look at each other, at us, nostrils flared. Their teeth clenched in rictuses of hate.

Then one of them lets Redfearn go. Another.

The motors of their boats chug. They back out and away, droning into the gathering night. Their eyes watching us as they leave, promising vengeance.

Then they're gone, leaving the bay silent again but for the gentle lap of water. The crews of the yachts watching us.

Redfearn and I let out a long, low whoosh of air.

I'm shaking, trembling like a leaf, the drop in adrenaline leaving me light-headed. When I rise to my feet on wobbling legs, Redfearn pulls me into his embrace. "It's okay," he whispers in my ear. "We made it."

I cling to him, my throat blocked up, and try to still my trembling. I can't believe it. We did. We survived.

At least, we survived that.

Now for what's ahead.

"When ready," the boatman says behind us. He's gesturing toward his little boat rocking in the water beside the boulder, a black-lacquered little sampan just narrow enough to squeeze through the tunnel.

The boatman in his black Chinese tunic eyes us up and down. Our yachtie clothes. The blood splattered all over us. "Please change into more . . . *suitable* attire."

For a moment, I want to laugh. Here. Now. Bloody and reeking of smoke, and he wants us to follow dress code.

But I don't laugh. Because it's more than a request. It's a reminder of what's coming.

Of what we have to do next.

In the end, it has a sobering effect on us. We nod and trudge into the tender's pop-up cabin. We move slowly, slump-shouldered, like revelers exhausted after a long night out. Redfearn doesn't seem to register anything he's looking at until he sees the bridal gown the Steward gave me, half-shoved into its box again. His face turns to stone. "I suppose you'll be wearing that."

The twist of jealousy in the words is plain. And I know how to appease it. I can't help but let a tired grin steal across my face as I open a case that's different from the weapons cases, turn about to hold up two sets of clothing in dry-cleaner plastic.

"Actually, I had Chung's men drop these off for us. I thought we'd dress like ourselves tonight."

And Redfearn's lips part as he takes in the black gala tux in my left hand, and in my right—a gorgeous and custom-made qipao.

I meet his eyes, my smile fading as my voice grows serious. "Let's go gamble for your daughter's life."

PART SIX:

THE PALACE

OF THE FANG

TWENTY-FIVE

The boatman motors us toward the tunnel leading to *The Palace of the Fang*.

Redfearn and I stand side-by-side at the bow watching the tunnel mouth loom before us, fanged with stalactites, braziers set into the cliff face blazing like eyes. The captain looks resplendent in his tuxedo. The blood has been washed from his face, his salt-and-pepper hair swept back from his brow in a gleaming wave, his shoulders broad and square in his suit. He still has a slew of cuts and bruises on his face from all our scrapes over the past couple of weeks, but it doesn't matter. He's still devastatingly dashing.

And he can't keep his eyes off me. The qipao I'm wearing. That handsome face filled with astonishment that I'm wearing it.

And for a moment, I can see myself through his eyes.

The qipao is stunning. Bare-backed, hugging my curves, embroidered and damasked with an Oriental dragon, a roiling of flame and golden coils wrapping about me. For a long time now, I have thought myself as cold as my name. But I don't feel anything cold about me in this moment. I am exploding with color and passion.

I hadn't known what I thought I'd feel, donning a qipao again. Miss Wang had been right. I'd allowed my husband to make me feel ashamed of my heritage. But it's not shame I'm feeling now. Nor do I feel that I have somehow capitulated, wearing—if not the bridal gown—another thing that he would enjoy.

I'm wearing this for me.

I'm wearing this to come home.

I'm wearing this to come into my power.

And that *is* what I feel. Pride. And power. And resolution.

We are going to get Penelope back. One way or another. And I am going to face my fears.

I am, finally, going to become more than them.

"You look amazing," Redfearn whispers, staring at me, and I flush as we float into the tunnel.

Darkness falls over us, the twin lanterns bobbing on poles at the sampan's bow flickering on the rock walls. There's a rustling above our heads. The chittering of bats, eyes glittering as they hang from the tunnel ceiling. I shiver, a sudden fear creeping up my spine, and Redfearn slides his hand into mine.

Of course, he has his own fears, too.

I catch his eye, my hand squeezing his. Telling him: *I believe in you. You can do this. You can get your daughter back. Something good will come of that gambling addiction. You won't let it destroy you now.*

He squeezes my hand in return, giving me a tender, tentative smile as we glide out of the far end of the tunnel.

We both face what's waiting for us.

The Palace of the Fang is otherworldly. As Redfearn told me, it's a barge that's been transformed into a three-story floating casino. But he didn't tell me just how magnificent it is. It's like something out of one of my father's folk tales: a palace of light, glowing like a vision on a lake in an open cave. All horned roofs and red gables lit by neon lights, torches and charcoal braziers. Not to mention the hundreds of paper lanterns floating on the dark water about it like a sea of souls.

Fireworks explode in the night sky above. Their blinding flash turns the lake into a pane of roiling flame, illuminating the cave walls soaring around us. And what's hanging from them.

They're coffins. Hundreds of them, resting on beams jutting out from the cliff face. Primitive boxes scrawled in gaudy calligraphy and splattered with white streaks of birdshit. Some tilting precariously, ready to slide out of their berths and crash into the lake. Others so old they look as if they date back to before the imperial dynasties of ancient China. And all of them containing the guardians of the casino. Lids crack, and from those slits of darkness glowing eyes peer at us, raising the goose bumps on my bare arms.

And the glittering showers of fireworks rain down lower, illuminating the person waiting for us on the casino's stoop above the landing stage.

It's Hong.

The owner of *The Palace of the Fang* appears to have survived his boat crash and been returned to his place of business. He stands in a fresh suit with legs spread, his hands bunched at his sides. He has a bandage of white gauze taped to the left side of his head, over his ear. Its center is soaked red through with blood.

I wonder what that ear looks like under that gauze. I know it will be healing at a supernatural rate, as I've seen Adrian's wounds do. I wonder if it will completely reform, or end up as a grotesque knob of scar tissue.

I know which he deserves.

He glares down at us as Redfearn hops aboard the landing stage, offers me a hand. The vampire's eyes glow from the braziers and floating candles, hot with murder. They linger on me, making it clear that he hasn't forgotten, that his vengeance won't be denied. Then they swing to Redfearn, promising a much more imminent vengeance.

He forces a sickly polite smile. "Welcome to *The Palace of the Fang.*"

Redfearn offers me an arm, waits for me to thread mine through it, and then deigns to respond as we start up the stairs toward Hong. "I see the Steward sent his errand boy again to fetch us."

Hong's expression curdles. "I'd disembowel you where you stand if I could."

Redfearn raises his brows. "At least your greetings are improving. I'm impressed." He stops us on the stoop before Hong and pauses. "Well? Are you going to let us in?" He snaps his fingers. "That's right, I forgot. Must be suffering from some hearing loss."

Hong's eyes blaze. He hisses, lips snarling back from his teeth, baring a pair of freakishly long fangs. And he takes a step toward us, hands curled into claws.

The sound of a hundred coffin lids creaking open roots him to the spot.

All around us, eyes peer down at us from those coffins hanging high above. The coffin dwellers have pushed their lids all the way back with splayed and spidery hands, have sat up to grip the rims of their boxes. Fireworks explode in the darkness above the palace's horned towers, and that sudden glare reveals gray and laddered skin, fangs as bright as new-minted steel, eyes flashing like coins in sunken sockets.

Redfearn cocks his head and smirks. "Forget your own rules, Mr. Hong? No blood spilled on palace grounds, remember?"

Hong clenches his teeth, the skin tightening across his brow. But he slowly continues forward, hands open in a gesture of good faith—and begins to pat Redfearn down. "You are a lucky man, Captain Redfearn," he snarls, low enough that only we can hear.

Redfearn stares straight ahead. "Let's hope so."

Hong removes the Heckler & Koch P30 from Redfearn's tuxedo jacket, hefts it. "You thought I'd let you back into my establishment without searching you?"

Redfearn slides his jaw from side to side but says nothing.

Hong smirks. "No," he says, tossing the pistol to one of the guards. "Can't be giving you an unfair advantage at the gaming table, can we?"

"That afraid your boss is going to lose, are you?"

Hong, patting down Redfearn's arm, pauses to squeeze the captain's stitched-up wound through his tux.

Redfearn sucks in air between his teeth. Hong, eyes glittering with malicious gratification, moves on to me.

He's not modest about it. He slides his hands down my sides, tracing my hips in lingering, sleazy enjoyment, and Redfearn's lips thin. "Watch it," he growls.

Hong's hands freeze on my thigh. He arches a brow and pulls out my little five-shot revolver from my thigh holster. "I see the familiar isn't without bite herself." He tosses the gun, moves onto my other thigh. Both eyebrows shoot up now as he unsheathes the push dagger, admires the flash of steel in the light of the braziers. His eyes find mine. "Well, well. You're packing an awful lot for a chief stew." His eyes narrow. "I can see why the Steward is obsessed with you."

Redfearn inhales noisily through his nose. "Are we quite done?" He makes a curt gesture. "Shall we?"

Hong smirks, his eyes remaining on me, but spins on his heel to fling up a hand. A pair of bodyguards step forward to open the double doors of the casino. These doors are not fashioned for mortals. They're rounded, adorned in a fantastical ivory design that evokes a fiendish ingrinning of teeth. A celebration of fangs.

Those teeth part, and then Hong is leading us into *The Palace of the Fang*.

Redfearn catches my eye as if to steady me. I wince a smile and pull close, locking my arm tightly through his. I feel strangely naked and helpless without the weapons on my thighs, and my courage wavers. Whatever flimsy illusion of safety I'd had, it's gone now. That's been stripped from me.

But I won't let that stop me. All the paths in my life have led me here, and I can't turn from it now.

We stride through the doors.

It's all a blur. A fever dream of seductive red light, gambling tables glowing under Chinese lanterns. The indistinct faces of women pass me, and I know they're the currency here. They are the stakes. And all of them wear qipaos. Their eyes flick to me, dark brown, the lids curved upward at the corners. A look of recognition. My chest thrums, heavy with a feeling of kinship, an unexpected bond that steels my will. I straighten my spine and keep my eyes on the black shape of Hong's back as he leads us through the crowd, feeling the eyes of those in suits watching me, the quivering pulse of an artery at my throat. We pass cedar columns, wall panels embossed with the gilt figures of mythical creatures, and then we're ascending a staircase banistered with carved dragons.

Something about going up those steps, reminding me of how close we are, changes everything. Dread pools in me, sapping my strength. I feel sick to my stomach. I am gripped with the sudden certainty that this is a mistake.

I cannot do this. I'm not ready for this.

I'm not ready to face him.

But it's too late. The blur that's Hong leads us into a private room and steps side. There's a stand of wooden screens here bearing murals of bloodthirsty seascapes: red waves, floating coffins, evening skies plagued by bandy-winged things. And there's a poker table, its top upholstered with crushed red velvet. Penelope Redfearn sits at the table, facing us. I see, with a sick pang in my gut, that she's wearing a qipao, her blond hair done up in a tight bun, like mine. She looks like a doll.

On her shoulder rests a pale hand. A man's hand. Long fingers crowned with horny nails. The claws of a beast.

The Steward of Castle Volok stands behind Penelope.

He smiles. "I'm glad you could make it."

TWENTY-SIX

Redfearn takes a step forward, emotion lurching into his face. "Pen . . ."

"Daddy," she whispers, eyes welling, and strains forward for a moment, as if to stand. But the Steward's hand is there on her shoulder. It squeezes down hard. Those talons dig into flesh, and Penelope flinches and falls silent, biting her lip.

Redfearn swallows, his face aching. "It's okay, sweetheart. I'm going to get you out of this. I'm going to take you home."

"Are you?" The edges of the Steward's mouth sneak upward. Tonight, he wears a bowtie and a stunning red tuxedo jacket emblazoned with dragons and roaring flames. It makes him glow. "I've heard you are quite the poker player. We will see if you're that good."

Redfearn's eyes slowly roll up to the Steward. His jaw works side to side, teeth grinding.

The Steward, smirking, sidles his eyes to me.

"My, my," he marvels, appraising my qipao with its brilliant coruscation of golden dragon scales. "I see that you have finally embraced yourself again." Then his eyes go to my bare neck, pointedly drop to the blood ring on my hand. Finally, his gaze lifts to mine. "It suits you. All of it."

A wave of humiliation washes over me. I blink and take a breath, lift my chin.

This is my choice, I tell myself. *I do not belong to him. I never will again.*

His eyes glow.

At length, he extends a hand toward the chairs nearest us. "Please."

Redfearn, muscles still flexing at the corners of his jaw, pulls out a chair for me, then sits beside me. The Steward claims a seat beside Penelope, and then Hong joins on our right. It is all a joke. A comedy. An elaborate farce we all know hides a squirming rot beneath.

I feel myself poised on a dizzy brink, buffeted by shame and terror. The enormity of what will be decided at this table—and within the next hour—is almost too much to take in properly. It's dangerous to even try.

"Ladies and gentlemen," Hong says, taking out a fresh deck of cards and beginning to shuffle. "The game is no-limit hold 'em. Five communal cards, two in the hole, ten million dollar buy-in. The game is over when one player loses all his chips, whereupon the real stakes are won. We all know what those are."

Penelope and I lock eyes across the table.

"Anyone who forfeits the game forfeits their stakes. And anyone who tries to flee the premises before the game is over will be met by the mercy of the palace guardians. Are the rules clear?"

Penelope and I nod. Redfearn and the Steward don't—they've locked eyes as if locking horns.

"Then let us begin."

Hong deals out three community cards face-up in a row before him, then two face-down to both Redfearn and the Steward. The Steward tips up the ends of his and examines them with the studious calm of a mortician. He has a hell of a poker face.

Redfearn doesn't look at his right away. He's watching the Steward.

The Steward glances up, catching Redfearn watching. His lips twitch.

Then Redfearn looks down at his cards as if they're a tumbler of whiskey.

I know what he's going through. I can see it in his face. The struggle. The fear of what will happen if he begins. If he'll be sucked under by that old addiction in him, that curse that's been patiently biding its time these past few years, waiting to overthrow all reason again.

Under the table, I place my hand on his knee: *I believe in you*.

It's enough. Taking a deep breath, the captain places a hand on the cards, his fingers tracing—for the briefest of moments—along the textured design of them, as if getting reacquainted with old friends.

Then he tips up their ends to peek at what he has: a red nine and seven.

He has nothing.

The Steward's eyes take on a gloating gleam.

He slides a short stack of chips across the red felt and the betting begins. Two more cards are added to the common cards, and there are two more rounds of betting, with the pot getting up to six million. Redfearn now holds two pair, nines and sevens. But I know the Steward most likely has a better hand. He operates with the precision of a pro. He handles his cards, stacks his chips, and moves his eyes in small, efficient manners, all with the stoicism of a cobra. I can tell that Redfearn is no less experienced, but his style is a little rougher around the edges. More importantly, I know he's not thinking clearly. He keeps meeting the Steward's bets and raising them, and when the Steward drops his hand on Penelope's bare knee, the muscles around Redfearn's eyes contract.

"You have a very special daughter, Captain Redfearn," he remarks, stroking the backs of his fingers up and down Penelope's thigh. "I can see why you'd be so reluctant to allow another man to have her. She is quite . . . gifted."

Penelope drops her head, cheeks burning with shame. Redfearn's fist tightens around a handful of chips, scraping and grinding them together like stones as his knuckles bulge.

"I'm sorry, Daddy," Penelope breathes, her voice wet with a held-back sob.

The Steward places a hand on the back of her neck, massaging it as if in comfort. It does not look comforting.

"Don't worry, captain. I will make her very happy." The Steward smirks. "I *have* made her very happy."

It happens before I can stop it. Redfearn shoots out of his chair, teeth clenched, and I grab his arm. "Redfearn!"

The Steward is giving the captain a sleek and oily smile, as if he has won a small victory. He adds a heavy gaming plaque onto the pile: another million.

Hong turns a carefully placid face to Redfearn. "Your bet, captain."

Redfearn is trembling, his blazing eyes trying to bore a hole through the Steward's face, and I can suddenly see it. The gambler he was. That fatalistic addiction driving him to go all in, never stopping when he knew he should.

And that was without this rage.

I place a hand on his, lean to whisper into his ear. "Redfearn. You know he probably has a full house with that hand. Don't do it. He's trying to get into your head. Don't let him."

With a mighty effort, he turns to look at me, and I shake my head. "You can't afford to lose anymore. Not with what's at stake."

He looks at Penelope's hung head, the tears slipping down her cheeks.

His lips peel back from his teeth.

Slipping his hand out from under mine, he grabs a gaming plaque and tosses it onto the pile, tosses his two cards over. "Call," he growls.

A slow, revolting smile creeps across the Steward's face, and he slides his eyes to me.

My skin grows cold, and I slowly sink back into my chair. I already know.

The Steward turns his cards over, and Hong drags them to him, pushes three common cards forward. "Royal flush. The Steward wins."

The captain stares at the cards as if not seeing them. The Steward looks up at him, his tone cheerful, accommodating. "Would you like a drink, captain?"

Redfearn drags his eyes to the Steward, sinks back into his chair and watches as the vampire drags the pile of chips toward him and begins stacking them.

My head buzzes. I take a breath, rallying myself. "That's all right. We can come back from that—"

"I spotted his tell."

I still all over. "What?"

Redfearn leans to whisper in my ear, the faintest trace of a smile about his lips. "He fidgets with his chips when he has a good hand."

I pull back enough to look into his eyes, and it dawns on me: *He was bluffing*.

It was all a show. He was pretending to fall prey to his addiction so he could figure out his opponent.

Redfearn leans away, his face slipping once more into a mask of defeat.

My chest thrums. He hasn't lost himself. He's not let himself be outsmarted.

Maybe he has more of a chance than I thought.

Hong deals again. Redfearn gets an ace of hearts, which makes it a pair with one of the common cards. The

Steward, flush with triumph, starts laying into Redfearn again: If it worked once, it will work again.

"I've been wondering how good you'd be at this. If I had to confess, I'm a little disappointed."

He pushes a stack of chips into the middle. One hundred thousand. Redfearn lets his teeth clench again and meets it.

The Steward, smirking, continues. "Maybe your reputation is all talk?"

With the turn card, Redfearn gets three aces.

Penelope watches him, her chest rising and falling in quick, shallow breaths.

"Watch closely, my dear." The Steward's teeth show as he fidgets with his chips, sliding one up and around a stack of three in his hand, over and over, in an endless loop. "Look at who your father is."

He pushes forward three stacks of chips this time. Again, an angry-looking Redfearn meets it. He has almost no chips now.

The final card, and Redfearn is rivered into a full house: aces full of kings.

Redfearn watches the Steward. When he gets his card, Volok's underling stills, fingers poised: He is no longer fidgeting with his chips.

He's not overly pleased with his hand.

The Steward lifts his eyes to Redfearn now. To anyone watching, it would look like Redfearn is sweating with anger, having lost himself in his rage.

Which means that he looks like he's ready to risk it all again, even if it means trying to bluff his way there with a bad hand. And that whatever unimpressive hand the Steward has would still be better.

The Steward tosses a gleaming plaque onto the pile. "I raise you one million."

Redfearn glares at him, slides his gaze to Penelope. Her eyes plead at him, and for a moment they are once more the eyes of a little girl. The eyes of a daughter. "Get him, Dad."

A muscle jumps at the corner of his eyelid. He looks on the verge of losing it.

He counts the rest of his chips. Then he triangles his hands around a stack and slides it forward, sweeps all his remaining chips into the middle in a noisy, clattering cascade. "All in. Raise you two million and three hundred thousand."

The Steward narrows his eyes, studying him, and Redfearn glares back. Penelope holds her breath. I hold mine.

At length, a smile jags across the Steward's mouth. He's bought it. He thinks Redfearn can't help himself again. "Very well." He pushes a mound of his own chips into the middle. "If you insist on losing everything in your life." He settles back into his seat, his voice lazy with scorn. He tilts his head slightly to include Penelope. "Witness your father throw you away with his anger, my dear." He juts his chin. "Call."

Redfearn's demeanor suddenly changes. All the anger drains out of him. His face slackens. His shoulders drop. He goes cool and collected.

He tosses his two cards over.

The Steward stares. He blinks and leans forward, as if having to double check what he's seen, and his eyes go round. Then he flashes a look at Redfearn. The wrathful look of a man who has been bamboozled and betrayed.

At last, his lips thin. He picks up his two cards and flicks them across the table.

Hong clears his throat. "Your win, Captain Redfearn."

I let out a breath I didn't know I was holding. Penelope, lips parted and brow furrowed, stares at her father as if she doesn't recognize him. As if, all this time, she hasn't seen this person before.

And, indeed, Redfearn looks completely changed. He drags all the chips toward his side of the table, begins to stack them in calm and unruffled silence, as if he had known—all along—it would play out this way.

The Steward stews. He eyes his measly stack of remaining chips, his mouth quivering, his fangs pressing down into the meat of his bottom lip, giving him a rather dimwitted look. He rolls his gaze at Redfearn.

"I suppose you think you're rather clever."

Redfearn ignores him, stacking his chips.

"I suppose you think this makes a difference. That I didn't let you outplay me. That you actually have a chance to get your daughter back."

But these taunts no longer have any effect on Redfearn. The captain arranges his chips into tidy rows. It's as if the Steward doesn't exist.

And I see it work its way to the front of the Steward's consciousness: He *was* outplayed. He didn't know the caliber of the player sitting across from him. He didn't know my man.

He knows he's already beaten.

So he resorts to the only thing he can do.

He edges a look at Hong, gives an almost imperceptible nod. An understanding passes between them. A prearranged decision. The owner of *The Palace of the Fang* nods back.

He shuffles and begins to deal. And when he gets to the Steward—it's almost too fast to register—he deals from the bottom of the deck.

The world blurs.

My ears ring. Sounds have become muffled: the snap of cards, the tenor of voices. Someone is speaking, but I do not catch the words. Because the skin on my scalp has gone crawly and strange. Because a terrible knowledge has poured into my body, scalding it from the inside out. The knowledge that there's no way Redfearn can win now. Everything is now stacked against him, and bit by bit Hong and the Steward will take him apart.

I can see it now. The helplessness of it, Redfearn wheezing with useless rage as he is slowly divested of his chips. As he realizes that—no matter how good his cards are—there's no hope of ever getting his daughter back.

A cruel and drawn-out humiliation that he will never recover from. Penelope weeping and sobbing as she's dragged away from him, as I'm dragged away from him. And him going back to the bottle for the rest of his days, dying one night of a failed liver in an alley somewhere, or from a flash of fangs.

I can't make him go through that. I can't make any of us go through that.

I know what has to happen next.

I study the side of Redfearn's face. That face I know so well. It's so close, it wouldn't take much at all for me to lean and kiss his bristly cheek.

A part of me does kiss his cheek. A part of me kisses him and says, *I'm right here, Redfearn. I will always be right here.*

I place my hand over his, squeeze it, and he looks at me, brows knitted in confusion.

I love you. I will always love you.

Then I'm rising from my chair, my knees wobbly. The room grows quiet, but I am not here. A part of me is back with Redfearn when he told me he loved me. A part of me is lying in bed and listening to him whisper, *My sailor moon.*

"Yes?" The Steward raises his brows. The word mocking, but curious.

"Mrs. Colding," Redfearn says, a concerned and almost frightened note in his voice.

I am yours, Redfearn. I always will be.

I clear my throat. "All right," I declare to the room.

The Steward lifts a brow. "All right what?"

And Redfearn looks at me in that glow of bioluminescence, when he dove off his efoil to save me. We are bobbing in that magical swirl of light and I am falling in love with him all over again.

Forgive me. It has to be this way. This is the only way.

I chuck up my chin and say it. "You can have me again in exchange for Penelope."

TWENTY-SEVEN

Redfearn shoots to his feet, his face wiped of all expression. Slowly, his brows pinch together. A look of sorrow and confusion and, behind that, the woundedness of the betrayed. Even the suspicious. "What are you—"

"It's all right," I tell him, heated shame creeping up the back of my neck, and touch his arm. "It's best this way."

Is he thinking what I'm thinking? Does he wonder—deep down—that there's more to this than self-sacrifice? That this is all too convenient?

He shakes his head, his whole body trembling, his mouth scrunching up in denial. "No . . . no . . ."

And I wrap my arms around his neck, hold him close. My mouth to the shell of his ear. "I love you."

He lets out a harsh, ragged breath and holds me tight, crushing me to him. His voice drawn out of him as if from the roots of a mountain. "I love you, too."

We draw back and look into each other's eyes. He places a callused hand to my cheek. "You always have to do things your way, don't you?"

The corner of my mouth tugs, and I reach up to grip his hand. "Always."

We stand there, unable to let go, all the moments of our romance rushing through our eyes, leaving our throats too lumped up to speak.

He can't do it. He opens his mouth to try again—

But there's the creak of a chair, a body shifting.

When we turn to the Steward, his full lips wear a slick smile of victory.

He rises, a hand on Penelope's shoulders. She's trembling, looking from me to Redfearn, her lashes batting as if unable to process what is happening. The Steward guides her around the red-felted gaming table and stops her, draws her into a close embrace. "You know how much I'll miss you."

She stands there with her arms at her sides, stiff as a doll.

He releases her, urges her forward.

She tries to keep it together; it lasts only for a moment. She rushes into her father's arms and clings to him, her cheek pressed into his shirt, blotching it with her tears. "Daddy," she chokes, and Redfearn's eyes fill, his mouth quivering. He strokes her hair. "My little sun."

I have to hold back a prickling of tears.

Then Penelope is turning to me. She wipes at her face and looks up into my eyes. She opens her mouth. "Mrs. Colding, I—"

"It's okay." I smile and chuck up her chin with the crook of a finger. "I'll be okay. I promise."

Her eyes dart back and forth, searching mine. They go glassy again, and she draws me into a sudden, hard hug, her head pressed against my collarbone. I wrap my arms around her.

"Thank you," she whispers.

Then she's stepping back, and Redfearn is holding her hand, both of them looking at me. A life apart.

I work the lump out of my throat. "You promise they'll have safe passage out of here."

The Steward, eyes glinting, inclines his widow's peak. "You have my word."

Hong extends a pale hand, bowing slightly at the waist to Redfearn and Penelope. "I'll see you to your boat."

He strides from the room, and then Penelope is passing me. Redfearn—my love—is passing me. His hand brushes mine, fingers curling around mine for the briefest of moments. A touch that sparks. That scars.

Then he's gone.

I close my eyes, the room suddenly dizzy. My hearts feels as if it has lurched out of my chest after him, slapped onto the floor. Useless.

There's no use for it anymore, after all.

When I open my eyes again, the Steward stands before me.

He looms. I can see the glint of his teeth, pinching his bottom lip in that feebleminded look. His eyes. The engulfing wells of them—commanding, annihilating—as he looks down at me.

His lips twitch in a smile. "My little empress."

And I shiver, as if those words were a touch on my skin. A violation, claiming me.

That smile widens, taking on new hints of sinister meaning, sparkling with malice. He hooks his chin. "After you."

I turn, head high, and step from the room. I cannot feel the floor under me. I can hear the click of my heels, feel a cold hand on the small of my back, ushering me onward. To oblivion. To hopelessness.

The stairs, descending. A clamor of voices. Staring eyes. The glow of passing lanterns. A life passing.

I need to start. I need to speak.

I find my voice again. "What now?" I ask.

"Now, we rediscover our marriage," the Steward purrs beside me, his voice smooth with smug self-assurance. "Now, we go to my boat. It is nothing to boast of, a mere placeholder after . . . well, you took both the boat and the house, didn't you? But do not worry. I will commission another one from the Shipwright, something more appropriate for our new life together. We will have a home again. Perhaps we'll even go back to Colding Mansion. I'm sure we can make it suitable once more."

A chill touches my throat.

As we walk, his hand traces up my bare back in my qipao, making the fine hairs there stand on end. That hand comes to rest on the back of my neck and begins to caress, just as it caressed Penelope. The heavy, possessive weight of a predator. A finger traces my fang-mark scars, and I suppress a shiver, thinking of my dream. Of his fangs sliding into those scars, eliciting a long moan of pleasure from me.

Doubt muddles everything. The notion—the fear—that I wanted this.

This is my chance, I know. If that were true. If a damaged part of me always yearned to go back to him. To have that life again. The twisted comfort—the familiarity—of that life again.

All I'd have to do is keep following him.

My mouth has gone dry.

A hallway now, lined with terracotta warriors. These warriors do not look normal. Their mouths are carved with fangs.

Ahead, the round double doors of the palace.

I do not have much time.

"And you really think we can be happy again together?"

The question is light, carefully intonated, but I can feel his head turn toward me, his eyes crawling over my face. His voice drips certainty, condescension. "Happiness can be found wherever you're willing to find it."

Liars can speak truth, too.

But only when it serves them.

I think of what I said to Miguel. (*Take me away from this.*) And I know. I know I said that because, back then, I wasn't strong enough to do it myself.

But I'm not that person anymore.

"I don't know," I muse, my bottom lip pouting. "I worry."

His hand drops away at that. "Oh?"

I incline my head in a nod. "I worry that, after all the ways I've improved myself, you won't be man enough for me."

He halts before the doors. His eyes have narrowed, but I won't turn to him. I stare expectantly at the doors as if waiting for the guards to open them.

At last, he opens his mouth. "I don't really like your attitude right now."

And there it is, that phrase trained to bring on that paralyzing fear. And I do feel it. It bears down on me like that hand on my neck, clamping around my throat, choking off any impulse toward disobedience.

The Steward, satisfied, motions toward the guards. The doors are drawn back, and he steps through into the night.

Crisp, cool air blows on my face. I can hear the pop of those fireworks again. A fire like the one burning within me now, ready to burn away everything inside me that was cold. Everything that had frozen over. And I think of Miss Wang back in the Familiar Resort, and what she would say if she were with me now.

(Become who you are. Because we are stronger than them.)

And somewhere, deep inside, something cracks loose.

Time to embrace disobedience.

I lift my chin and step out to join him. "I'm not so sure," I announce with affected detachment. "You have become something of a failure."

The Steward rocks to a stop on the stoop overlooking the landing stage with all its waiting sampans. His hands claw into fists. His head twitches to the side. "What did you say?"

I clasp my hands before me and lift a brow. "Let me rephrase. Because you always were a failure, weren't you? A fraud. You inherited your wealth, were horrible at running your businesses. And now you lost your most important business, haven't you? Volok's castle. To me, I might add. You're of no use to Volok anymore. You have no purpose. And what is a man if he doesn't have purpose?"

The Steward turns about. His face is livid, his eyes full of that black void that, in the past, so utterly terrified me.

But I will not be cowed this time.

"How dare you—" he begins, lifting a long talon.

"You see, I rather fear I've outgrown you. All your flattery and sweet promises? For young, innocent, girls, they can be quite charming, I'll grant you. But for a full-grown woman? Well. Let's just say I know a thing or two now about manipulation."

He flies a look at the guards, the passing guests. When he gets to me, he snatches my hand, points a talon in my face. "Stop. Talking."

He starts down the stairs to the landing stage now, dragging me with him.

But I won't stop now. I'm just getting started.

"There's no hiding what you are now. I *see* you. You're not even a person. There's nothing there. You're empty."

I let out a peal of uproarious laughter, gesturing at his flashy tuxedo jacket with its glittering dragon designs. "You have to appropriate my culture to have some semblance of a personality. Our style. Our clothes. Even your blood sons were Chinese. You're a leech. A bloody colonizer. You're nothing."

He whirls, one hand blurring out to seize my face, fingers pinching my cheeks to hold me in place. His eyes glitter with violence. "I'm warning you."

But I shake myself loose and back away. We're both on the landing stage now. A stage for all to see. *The Steward vs. the chief stewardess*. The thought fills me with another sick urge to laugh.

Instead, I spread my arms, taking in the lit-up casino, the watching guests and boatmen. "What? Afraid to be embarrassed in front of your peers? But you never thought of them as peers, did you? No. You look down on them. You think you're superior, that you're better than everybody. When really, deep down, you know you're *nothing*." I take off my blood ring, hold it up for all to see before I drop it at my feet, crush it with the point of my heel and scrape it behind me, leaving a red smear on the wooden boards. "Well, I won't be owned by someone who's nothing. I won't be owned by anybody."

The Steward's eyes are huge, luminous with incandescent rage and disbelief. If he had blood moving in his veins, it would be flooding his face now. His rows of needle teeth clench, and he can't hold it back. He whirls, his hand blurring, and the smack across my face echoes across the lake.

I go down hard on the landing stage, the force of the impact jolting through my arm and hip bone. My cheek goes numb. My vision blurs, red dots dancing everywhere.

But I hear it.

The creaking up of hundreds of coffin lids.

All along the cliff walls surrounding the casino, the guardians of *The Palace of the Fang* are sitting up in their hanging coffins, spider fingers gripping lids, glowing eyes staring.

I can't stop now. Not when it's working. Not when his pride is beginning to undo him.

It's time to go all in.

I let out a cruel laugh that rings throughout the open cave. "Look at you," I gasp. "You're pathetic. I thought you chose me because I was weak. Because there was something wrong with me. I thought there was something broken in me to make me want to be with you. To make a part of me even now, God help me, want to go back to you. But now I know the truth. You're the one who's broken. You had to get me addicted to the highs and lows of your validation to distract me from the fact that you're incapable of love." I shake my head, flooded with a hot euphoria, all the years of silence and repression coming out of me in a rush of blinding release. "No. I know now. I know. You chose me because you knew, all along, that I was better than you. And you hated me for it."

Everything about the Steward goes taut as a violin string. He paces, dragging a hand through his slicked-back hair as he glances at everyone watching. He is burning with humiliation.

"Mr. Colding." It's Hong. He's starting down the steps, holding up a hand. "Mr. Colding, think about what you're—"

But I can't let him talk sense into the Steward now.

"What are you going to do?" I ask, lifting my chin, lips stinging. "You just gonna let them all see your wife humiliate you like this? You let your enemy and blood slave go so you could take back a wife who's going to disrespect you?" I cackle, the sound slapping flat and harsh off the cave walls. "And you think you really won?"

The Steward's eyelids contract to slits.

The slap smacks my face against the old boards of the landing stage, the force of the follow-through throwing him off-balance over me, long strands of black hair falling across his brow.

I see stars.

"Mr. Colding!"

But the Steward doesn't hear, doesn't see the guardians beginning to flow out of their coffins and down the walls of the cave.

He's too busy for that.

He slaps and slaps me, battering at my arms shielding my face, his talons drawing jagged gashes along my forearms. His lips peel back from his fangs as he snarls. "Fucking. Ungrateful. *Bitch!*"

And the guardians drop from coffin to hanging coffin, spring onto the horned towers of the casino, climb head-down along the rock walls like lizards and slip into the water. All of them converging on the landing stage.

Hong, face slack with fear, stops shouting and backs away, half stumbling, half clambering up the steps back to the casino.

But still the Steward is oblivious.

He seizes my wrists and jerks them down and away from my face, his eyes flat and black. The eyes of a psychopath. "I've been wanting to do this," he breathes, and tilts his head back to let his fangs inch farther out of his gums.

Terror leaps down my throat.

And that's when the horde of pale hands grab the Steward.

He's jerked away as if he'd never been there, and I lie there a moment, panting and uncomprehending. Then I hear the screams that make my blood freeze.

When I sit up, I see them.

There's so many crowding around the Steward that I can barely make him out. Dozens of them, gray and sunken-ribbed, flowing dripping out of the water to crouch over the former overseer of Castle Volok. Fireworks explode above the casino, igniting eyes in starved skulls into silver half-dollars. Claws gleam. Fangs flash as they rip and tear and nuzzle into flesh, drinking greedily. Taking one unsteady step closer, I catch a glimpse of the Steward's face. His brow has been gouged deep enough to show the glisten of bone beneath, a four-inch flap of skin with a bit of hairline attached to it hanging down, ruining that signature widow's peak. His ragged neck pulses blood, and he lifts a hand toward me, his vocal chords slashed and unable to produce a sound, a single noise of complaint. That voice that had so much power over me finally silenced.

I do not feel a thing.

A removed part of me thinks, *I guess that finalizes the divorce*.

When the feeding stops, all the crouching guardians swivel their glowing eyes toward me, blood dripping in long strings from their mouths.

My bones go cold.

Hong, pressed back against the casino steps, finds his voice again. "That's right! Her too!" He points a sharp finger. "That fucking bitch killed my son and blew up Castle Volok! She's a fucking traitor!"

I can see it in a glance: Their bloodthirstiness won't be stopped now. They can't help themselves. They abandon the ravaged, drained and shriveled thing that had once been my husband and rise up to their full height, eyes glittering like cold stars in their heads. They take a step toward me.

I retreat along the landing stage. The way back to the casino is blocked off. I've been backed into a corner. I have nowhere to go.

Fireworks boom and crackle overhead, silhouetting a small army of sinister shapes. They crouch like gargoyles on the casino's carved gables, crowd the palace grounds, flow down the steps and onto the landing stage.

They're everywhere.

"That's right, bitch," Hong taunts from the steps, laughing. "That's fucking right."

And they come on.

There's a splash of water and a grayish hand clamps around my ankle. One of them is behind me, coming up out of the lake. Its pitiful head all but bald and straggled with a few strands of lank black hair. It hisses.

My flesh crawls.

I let out a little cry of terror and kick at it, knocking it back into the water as I wrench my foot free. I land hard on my ass, my foot bare, the stiletto gone. I kick off the other stiletto and scramble up. My chest heaves, the breath shuddering in my lungs. Everything has been smeared into a jittery panic.

This wasn't how it was supposed to go. It wasn't supposed to end like this.

Blood pulses thick and red between the teeth of the guardians, dribbles onto wooden boards. The fireworks have stopped, and the night, suddenly, feels a lot darker.

Hong watches, eyes glowing with ecstatic triumph.

The closest guardian lifts a clawed hand.

I love you, Redfearn, I think, shutting my eyes.

And I hear it.

It's a low, electric drone that snaps my eyes open. All the heads of the guardians have whipped toward the mouth of the tunnel.

Because something impossible is flying out of it.

It's impossible because he's gone. He shouldn't be here. And because I know he hates those things with all his being.

But, just the same, Captain Arnold Redfearn flies out of the tunnel on an efoil board.

He couldn't have brought the tender; the tunnel was too narrow. So the efoil board was his only option. It's a joke. It looks ridiculous, something that should not be. But it's happening. All the same, it's happening. That motorized surfboard flies above the water as Redfearn carves through the votive candles floating on the lake. He raises his voice in a shout. "Get ready!"

Hong stiffens, springing to his feet now. "Fucking get her!"

The yacht captain arcs about to come alongside the landing stage, and the guardians see the danger now. They snarl, baring pink-stained teeth, and lunge for me with claws swiping—

But I've already jumped.

I land hard in Redfearn's arms. The impact knocks him off-balance, lurching the efoil away in a dangerous turn and sinking its mast deep into the water, and for a heart-stopping moment I think we're going into the lake. But somehow Redfearn rights us and we're speeding away, gliding above the water in a rush of air against my face. I hang onto the captain's neck and blink at him. "How—"

"Hang on."

He leans and we curve off across the lake undulating with guttering candles, dodging a guardian that's leapt at us from a cliff wall. Behind us, Hong is cursing, shouting himself hoarse, ordering boatmen to start their sampans after us. More and more guardians splash into the water around us, some of them swimming toward us silent as eels. But Redfearn deftly dodges them, making a beeline for the tunnel, and I think, *We've made it.*

Then the night is lit up by the thunderous rattle of machine-gun fire.

"Fucking kill them!" Hong screams, shrill and frantic.

Bullets whip past in a vicious crosshatching of orange light, ricochet off the cave walls in spits of sparks. Hong and the body guards have found their guns.

I clutch Redfearn. *Don't hit him*, I pray. *Please. Don't take that from me now.*

"I got you," Redfearn whispers.

He zigzags, veering away from the hot bodies of metal stitching up stammerings of light along the water, blurring past to bounce off rock. There's so many of them the cave wall in front of us looks to be made of sparkling birthday candles.

No, I think. *Please no.*

And then we're blasting into the darkness of the tunnel boiling with bats. They whirl and race about us in a panic, and I lower my head and huddle against Redfearn as we fly through them. A couple of them strike me, their felty wings flapping against my face with a soft, secret, feminine warmth. They're everywhere. The tunnel fills with their shrieks, the whine of errant bullets, and I whimper, huddling deeper into Redfearn's arms. He holds me tighter, shushing me. "Almost there," he growls in my ear, and I hear my father's voice again, tucking me into bed as a little girl, telling me I'll be safe from the monsters. Maybe I am. Maybe I can be again. The tunnel walls spark, the bats screech, and a ragged sob is building in my throat when we blast out of the far side of the tunnel, out into open air and freedom, bats gushing out after us into the night. I open my eyes to see the bay waiting for us, its water gleaming in the moonlight. And there ahead of us is a beaming Penelope waving from the helm of the amphibious tender. That tender that will outstrip any stupid sampan sent after us. That will bear us away to safety.

And I turn to look at Redfearn smiling down at me. His eyes twinkle. "I knew your plan would work," he says, his voice rumbling deep in his chest, vibrating against me. "But you didn't think I was going to leave my sailor moon behind, did you?"

I gape up at him, unable to speak. To voice my indescribable joy in this moment. And then Penelope is laughing, drawing a deep chuckle out of Redfearn, and I'm laughing, too. At the ridiculousness of it all. Me being in his arms on this silly efoil. My white knight on his shining and improbable steed. How we, somehow, pulled it off. It's done. We're free. I'm free.

I get to be with the love of my life. And I never have to be Mrs. Colding again.

I get to be me.

PART SEVEN:

MRS. REDFEARN

TWENTY-EIGHT

"Mrs. Redfearn?"

I jerk away from the canal to blink at the real estate agent holding the clipboard. "What?"

He studies me. He's middle-aged, with thinning, brownish hair, and the look is kind. "Still getting used to the name?"

I smile and reach up to hold the new half-moon pendant hanging around my neck. Not so long ago, that smile would have been a subtle twitch of my lips. But I feel it spread, warm and friendly, across my face. "I suppose so."

Something like understanding comes over his features, and he offers a pen. "Just sign here and it's done."

I take a moment to turn my gaze back to the canal. To where my husband's—*ex-husband's*—Sunseeker Predator yacht is being towed away by a boat from a marine salvage company. Its rust-stained brightwork glints in the failing, reddish light of sunset. The kind of sunset found only in Florida: exotic but deadly, tinged with decadence and violence. Maybe, I think, also with renewal.

When the yacht is gone and I'm certain I will never see it again, I turn to the offered clipboard and take the pen.

I lower the nib to the signature line at the bottom and hesitate. I'd almost signed with my old name.

Smiling to myself, I set nib to paper and scribble. I do not sign with a cold slash, as I used to. This name, this new identity, has broad, open strokes. A feeling of freedom.

The real estate agent takes the pen back.

Throughout the whole process, he hasn't asked many questions. Hasn't asked why I've taken so long to sell the place. Hasn't asked why I took the first offer presented to me and didn't try to get a better deal. He knows enough about life, I suppose, that he doesn't need to hear the answers. Perhaps he's gone through a divorce himself.

He tucks the pen into the pocket of his shirt. "How does it feel?"

I look up at Colding Mansion. Its rose stucco façade glows pink in the sunset, the withered bougainvilleas clinging to its towers and wrought-iron balconies making it look lonely and forlorn. Somehow sad.

I'm not.

"It feels . . . like spring."

The agent smiles to himself and taps the clipboard against his leg. "Well. I hope you enjoy retirement, Mrs. Redfearn."

I make sure to look him in the eye. "Thank you."

That smile changes, sending a slight heat into his cheeks, and he ducks his head and leaves me standing at the canal's edge. After a moment, I hear his voice again. "Afternoon, Mr. Redfearn. Ms. Redfearn."

I turn to find Redfearn and Penelope trudging across the lawn toward me. Once we got back to the States, the first thing Redfearn did was to bring Penelope to see her mother. There had been tears, and shouts of joy, and Margaret had given Redfearn such a tender look of gratitude that the former captain's eyes had glassed up, and I'd all but seen the years of guilt lift from his shoulders. Penelope stayed with her mother that weekend, and I'd expected the stay to be permanent. But to everyone's surprise—not least Redfearn's—Penelope had requested to stay with her father for the time being. And as I watch them now, there's a new closeness to them. He leans and say something to her, and she laughs in response.

I'm smiling again when they come up to me.

"Hello." His kiss is warm and bristly against my cheek, and he takes a step back to take me in, my vibrant qipao with its gold patterns. "I still don't recognize you."

I flush with pleasure.

Penelope feels the qipao's fabric between her fingers. "Is this a new designer? Where'd you get this one?"

I look down at the swirl of designs, smiling to myself. "A recommendation from a friend."

Redfearn's brows raise at this, but I give him a look that says, *Later*. Right now, I want answers of my own. I glance between the two of them. "So? How'd therapy go?"

They share a look, a shy smile at the edges of Penelope's lips. Redfearn answers for them, eyes crinkling with a secret joke. "It's a start."

Penelope and I share a look of our own now, one of many we've shared recently, and we don't need to say a word. Everything has been communicated.

"So?" Redfearn glances back at the driveway where his Jeep is parked, and where the real estate agent is pulling out in his shiny black Lexus. "You ready to say goodbye to yachting life?"

I turn to the sunset again and all that boundless sea beneath it, a wistfulness tugging at me. "Almost."

After this day, I know, I'll never step foot on a superyacht again. I'll never be whisked away on that heady high of adventure and wealth, of waking up every day in a new country but knowing exactly what I'll be doing that day. Because while the itinerary and demands of the owner and guests may change at the drop of a hat, the fundamentals of every day never change, never deviate. You are ensconced in a safety net of cleaning and guest service.

I try to convince myself that life on land won't be so bad. Maybe I'll never own a glass table, because I won't be able to stand the sight of all the fingerprints on it. I'll never be able to do laundry again without feeling the need to iron everything to perfection. But I'll be able to put a bottle in the fridge without its label facing outward. I'll be able to wear shoes inside. I'll be able to set something down on an open shelf without fear of it falling off in rough seas. And I won't have to call the chief engineer to fix something for me, because I now have a man in my life.

In the end, though, none of this matters, and I know that. Because that's not what I'll really miss.

I'll miss what my abuser gave me.

I'll miss the feeling of control.

On land, there would be no routine, no military-strict rules, no predictability. Every day would be a question mark. And there would be something terrifying about that.

There would be something freeing about that.

I hear the crunch of grass, and Redfearn slips his hand into mine and squeezes, the tenderness in the gesture bringing the sting of tears to my eyes. His thumb brushes the engagement ring he bought me the day we set foot on land again. "Change is good," he says. "Adrian's mansion in the Rockies will be a fresh start."

I try to swallow the lump in my throat. "I know. I just—need a moment."

His mouth curves in understanding, and we both stare out at the Atlantic. A balmy wind rises, sighing in the palm trees along the canal, bringing with it a perfume of salt, fish, sargassum and jet fuel, the faint scent of rotting citrus. Far off on the water, something white flashes. The fiberglass of a yacht hull. If you squint just right, it can almost be mistaken for the *Lair*.

My shoulders rise in a big breath, fall again as I let it out.

Redfearn turns to me. "Ready?"

I nod. "Just one more thing."

Redfearn and Penelope glance at each other, brows furrowed, and I reach up and pull out the pins in my severe bun, let my hair tumble down loose and flowy in the wind coming off the water.

When I turn to Redfearn and Penelope, they both have huge smiles on their faces.

"Now I'm ready."

Redfearn swallows, his eyes glistening. He wets his lips. "You look amazing, Mrs. Redfearn."

"Song," I correct him.

He cocks his head, and I look at him full in the eyes, a smile spreading across my face now. "My first name is Song."

His jaw drops a moment before he remembers and sucks it up again. His eyes are twinkling. He beams.

I take his hand. "Let's go to our new home, Arnold."

Penelope looks between us, her eyes dancing. We can't help it—we all laugh.

And with a last look at the sea, we're walking away and climbing into Redfearn's black Jeep, pulling out of the drive of Colding Mansion and leaving it behind forever. For a long time, I still fancy I can hear the sound of the sea in my ears. But eventually that's gone, too, because the Jeep's top is down and the wind is in my hair, blowing it behind me as Redfearn keeps glancing over at me as if I'm his treasure he will never let go. And all I can hear now is the wind and the music playing softly on the stereo, and we're talking and laughing as we drive west and away from all I was and toward what I'll be. Up into Colorado and the Rockies where a new life waits for us. A life without seawater and blood and fangs. A life I can make my own.

EPILOGUE

"Song! You're burning them!"

I throw up my hands as Penelope cuts in to take the bacon off the stove. "I surrender," I grumble, reminding myself—for the thousandth, grumpiest time—that I don't have to be perfect at everything. "I had a chef cook for me for twenty years. I don't know the first thing about working in a galley—I mean, a kitchen."

"You don't need to convince me." Penelope suppresses a snigger as she pokes the bacon with a ladle, and I swat at her. She giggles.

"Shouldn't you be doing your homework?" I grouse, a grin twisting my mouth.

"What with the disaster going on down here? I prefer having my new home *not* be burnt to the ground, thank you very much." She arches a brow, a twinkle in her eye that reminds me an awful lot of her father. "Shouldn't you be cleaning something?"

I give her a look. "Very droll, dear." I inhale through my nose, spread my hands and breathe out through my mouth like a yogi. "I am practicing cleaning the house only once a week."

A small smirk yanks Penelope's lips to one side, but her voice is serious. "I'm proud of you. Really."

I meet her eyes, feeling my face grow warm. "Thank you."

After a moment, she turns away to transfer strips of half-burnt bacon onto plates, her voice light and teasing again. "I think I even saw a muddy footprint by the door the other day."

"Okay, too far!" I say, closing my eyes and pretending to shield myself from her words as she erupts into a fit of laughter.

"Hey, it could be worse," she manages between breaths, hovering a ladleful of jiggling egg in the air. "At least I'm not 'accidentally' dropping things."

"Don't you *dare*," I warn, holding up an imperious finger, and she snorts laughter, grinning from ear to ear as she darts away from me to set the table.

A slight smile on my face, I plant my hands on my hips and watch her, enjoying the sound of her laughter. She's been doing so well lately. After three months of weekly therapy sessions both alone and with her father, I can't even recognize her. Her mood has brightened, that sour rebelliousness transformed into an industrious work ethic and an eagerness to learn at school, and she has more weight on her now, the bags gone from under her eyes. She prefers to wear long sleeves, hiding the scars on her arms, but you can barely see them now.

You can barely see mine, either.

I catch my reflection in the mirror above the stove, turn my head to admire the fang mark scars. They're silvery, pale as moonlight, and I no longer wake up from nightmares with them throbbing. I barely think at all of Adrian's kind anymore. Of Evangeline. Or the Steward and what happened.

I hope it's the same with Penelope.

As I rinse off the hissing bacon pan in the sink, I take in the mansion. It's done in that modern log style that makes it feel like a hunting lodge, a rack of deer antlers above the fireplace. The fire is low now, but Arnold will be in with more wood soon. We made it cozy, decorating it with mementoes from our yachting years and pictures of the wedding. The ceremony was small, nothing fancy like Arie and Adrian's. Just the five of us with Penelope as ring-bearer, in the woods behind the house, the branches of the pine trees strung with lights. I couldn't help myself and dipped back into chief stew mode, designing a nautical-themed tablescape that recalled a bioluminescent seafloor, a wedding cake decorated with a giant half-moon and a figure of a groom whisking a bride away on an efoil board. We spent the night laughing and catching up around a bonfire, and watching Arnold's carefree face in the glow of the flames had been a balm for my soul. No honeymoon yet, but we wanted to wait on that until we knew it would be safe to leave Penelope on her own for a couple of weeks.

How things can change. I thought it would take me a long time to get used to living on land again, let alone enjoy it. But within a month I was happier than I'd been in decades. Any worries I had of not being accepted by Penelope were instantly dispelled, and we soon got into a routine of cooking together, going out for walks in the mornings, watching a movie or playing board games at night.

We never play poker.

There's a part of me that's afraid all this will wear off. As if it's a dream, a vacation. That reality will set back in, and I'll be stranded once more in a terrible, yawning emptiness without purpose.

But it hasn't happened yet. And I have a feeling it won't.

Things are different now.

I wonder what's in store for us. We have enough money to never work again if we wanted to, thanks to our ridiculously generous retirement funds from Adrian. I have a feeling though that Arnold and I will want to put ourselves to use somehow. Maybe he'll want to teach efoil riding to the local cattle barons and fat cat retirees; he's taken it up recently, after all, as there are no waves to surf in Colorado's high mountain lakes. As for myself, maybe I'll want to volunteer somewhere, or go to school and become a counselor for domestic abuse victims.

For now, we're content with taking care of Penelope. That's where we're needed most. And that's all that matters.

For now, this alpine wilderness—where everything is wild and untamable—is the perfect antidote to my OCD.

I can survive with a little dirt in my life now.

The door opens, and a gust of winter wind seems to blow Arnold through it, guttering the flames in the hearth. He stamps the snow from his boots, tries to get the door with his arms full of wood. "Penelope," I say, and she rushes to close the door for him, shutting out the skirling white winds of the Colorado night. It's almost spring now, and the drifts are still here, bowing the trees and humped up high on the roadsides. The road leading to the house looks like a tunnel.

Arnold trudges across the living room and drops the wood onto the floor, begins chunking logs into the fireplace in flurries of sparks. I cross my arms, admiring him. He's grown out his stubble into a respectable silver beard, and with his plaid coat dusted with snow he looks like a lumberjack I wouldn't mind pouncing. And I have been. Every night.

"Bacon and eggs for dinner again?" he growls over his shoulder.

Penelope shrugs as she sets the table. "Song was cooking."

"Oh," Arnold says, dusting his hands. "I thought I smelled smoke."

Penelope twists her lips in a restrained smirk and throws a look at me. I point at her. "Don't even start."

Redfearn and Penelope glance at each other, then throw back their heads and laugh.

Thump, thump, thump.

We all freeze, the joyous mood in the house suddenly plunged into dread.

Redfearn and I lock eyes, our hearts racing double time. I know we're thinking the same thing.

They found us.

It's impossible. They shouldn't know where we are. They can't know. We didn't leave any loose ends. No one should have been able to track us here. The only people who know our whereabouts are Arie and Adrian.

But they've found us, all the same.

Good thing we put contingency plans in place.

Penelope looks between us. She's hugging herself, gripping her arms through her sweater where her scars are, and her voice is small and scared. "Do you think it's—"

"Penelope," Arnold says, placing his hands on his knees and rising. "Grab our bags from upstairs like we've talked about. Do it now."

Penelope backs away, throws us one last look at us before running upstairs. Then Arnold opens the closet by the door.

He hands me a Mossberg 590M 12-gauge shotgun and I do a push-pull check on the double-stack mag extending from its bottom, eye the ejection port to make sure the first shell is chambered like it should be. Arnold grabs the other Mossberg and does the same.

There's a thumping down the stairs and Penelope skids around the post at the bottom, bags in hand, her hair tucked behind her ears. She's thrown on a coat.

Arnold stuffs a pair of extra mags into the pockets of his coat. "I want you two to head out the back into the garage. If you don't hear from me in five minutes, take the Ford on the back road."

Penelope pulls a Glock out of her bag and flicks off the safety without looking at it. "We're not going anywhere."

Arnold looks at me, eyes pleading.

I shake my head.

The former yacht captain drops his eyes and snorts. "The women in my life."

Trembling smiles spread across our faces.

Then Arnold faces the door.

"Who is it?" he calls.

Outside, the wind howls, blasting icy snowflakes against the windowpanes. They sound like a thousand tiny daggers stabbing the glass.

No answer.

My heart thuds in my chest, making my throat ache. The Mossberg suddenly feels heavy as sin in my arms. Penelope drifts close, and I know what she needs. I rest the Mossberg upright against my shoulder and wrap an arm around her. She clings to me.

Arnold tucks the butt of his Mossberg against his shoulder, reaches out for the doorknob. He turns it.

Penelope's fingers bunch into my shawl, her body trembling against mine.

And Arnold flings the door open.

I hold my breath.

The door swings wide onto a rectangle of solid blackness. Flecks of white whirl in and out of it, a screaming void. Arnold's shoulders hunch as he aims his shotgun barrel into the night.

"Show yourself!"

The storm moans, whistling through the door and gusting snowflakes across the kitchen floor. The temperature in the room, suddenly, feels below freezing.

As our breath fogs in the cold, a crunching can be heard. Footsteps approaching.

Penelope's trembling body goes rigid. Arnold jerks his Mossberg level.

And a face appears out of the wintry gloom. Pale, bloodless. The flesh of the undead. Framed by the fur-trimmed hood of a heavy parka.

Its full, red lips move, revealing a pair of lovely fangs. "No need for that, Herr Redfearn."

The voice is cool, female, startlingly familiar. I know that voice.

It's German.

Arnold lets the barrel of his Mossberg droop as he peers at that shadowy face. *"Ilsa?"*

And the figure crosses the threshold into the light, pulling its hood back to reveal the exquisite features of the Shipwright of Transmarinia.

My heart skips a beat or three. Arnold's jaw drops. Penelope looks up at me, bewildered.

"But—but we went to your memorial—" Arnold sputters.

Ilsa Knackenkusser dismisses this with a wave of a pale, ungloved hand. "I'll explain, but we need to talk. It's not over."

Arnold's heavy brows push down. "What's not over?"

The Shipwright sighs, as if explaining to a child. "Volok. He may be gone, but his cultists are threatening Arie's reign." She sweeps her eyes around the room, letting them rest on my face. "And I need your help to find my partner they took from me."

ABOUT THE AUTHOR

D.V. Sullivan has been a deckhand in the Mediterranean, a bartender in New York and an English teacher in China. Now that he's no longer hosing salt off yachts during high-wind gales, he writes from his lair in the Pacific Northwest.

DVSullivan.com
Facebook.com/AuthorDVSullivan
TikTok @dvsullivanauthor
Instagram @dvsullivanauthor
X/Twitter @bydvsullivan